"I caught you at a vulnerable time, didn't I?"

Tessa tensed as Blaize walked slowly toward her. "Yessir, you did," she said flatly.

"On the rebound."

"More or less."

He kept coming. "I won't say I'm sorry, Tessa." He slid his arms around her and drew her into a loose embrace. "And I won't accept that you don't want anything more to do with me. We're good together."

"In bed, sir. That's all."

"That's a start." He pulled her closer.

Tessa found the presence of mind to press her hands against his chest and push herself back. "More like a finish, sir."

"Not for me, it isn't."

EMMA DARCY nearly became an actress until her fiancé declared he preferred to attend the theater *with* her. She became a wife and mother. Later, she took up oil painting—unsuccessfully, she remarks. Then she tried architecture, designing the family home in New South Wales. Next came romance writing—"the hardest and most challenging of all the activities," she confesses.

Books by Emma Darcy

HARLEQUIN PRESENTS
1351—ONE-WOMAN CRUSADE
1385—THE COLOUR OF DESIRE
1401—RIDE THE STORM
1433—BREAKING POINT
1447—HIGH RISK
1455—TO TAME A WILD HEART

HARLEQUIN ROMANCE
2900—BLIND DATE
2941—WHIRLPOOL OF PASSION
3085—PATTERN OF DECEIT

Don't miss any of our special offers. Write to us at the following address for information on our newest releases.

Harlequin Reader Service
P.O. Box 1397, Buffalo, NY 14240
Canadian address: P.O. Box 603,
Fort Erie, Ont. L2A 5X3

EMMA DARCY

the wedding

Harlequin Books

TORONTO • NEW YORK • LONDON
AMSTERDAM • PARIS • SYDNEY • HAMBURG
STOCKHOLM • ATHENS • TOKYO • MILAN
MADRID • WARSAW • BUDAPEST • AUCKLAND

Harlequin Presents first edition June 1992
ISBN 0-373-11463-X

THE WEDDING

Printed in U.S.A.

CHAPTER ONE

HOW COULD HE?
  How could he!
The refrain had pounded through Tessa's head all night. It had punctuated the rattle of the train trip to North Sydney from her sister's home in Chatswood. It was still throbbing through her mind as she entered the huge CMA building that housed the headquarters of Callagan, Morris and Allen, the engineering and architectural company that claimed her services as a secretary.

That any man—but most particularly a man who said he loved her—could do such a thing! It was beyond Tessa's comprehension.

Tears pricked her eyes again. She determinedly blinked them back as she strode across the foyer. No more tears for Grant Durham. He didn't deserve them. He didn't deserve anything from her, ever again!

She entered an empty elevator and jabbed the button for her floor. As the doors closed she vehemently vowed she would close the door on Grant Durham and never let him back into her life. Never!

She had issued the ultimatum last night. Out! And if Grant was not out of her apartment by the time she got back after work today, she would—she would... Well, she didn't know what she would do, except the scene that would follow would be dreadful.

Her stomach twisted. Her heart ached. Her mind reeled weakly for a moment, then clutched at an even fiercer self-determination.

The elevator reached her floor and Tessa stomped down the wide corridor to Jerry Fraine's executive suite of offices, stoking resolution with righteous and furious indignation as she reviewed the degrading humiliation of the previous evening. No more pain, she told herself. No more anguish over him. Grant Durham was finished. FINISHED! In her mind's eye the word looked better in capital letters. No forgiveness. Not for any reason. Never. Four years of her life she had wasted on him, on and off, but this was THE END! Not another day more!

She threw open the door to her own little office and hurled it shut behind her. That made her feel better. She needed to give some vent to the churning emotions she had been trying to contain. Converting pain into anger was very good therapy. Tessa tried a bit more of it.

She threw her weekend bag into the corner beside the filing cabinet. She opened the large bottom drawer of her desk, dropped her handbag in, kicked the drawer shut. She opened the top drawer, snatched up the keys to the filing cabinet and banged that drawer shut as well. She unlocked the top file drawer, withdrew the folder of reports to be processed and slammed the drawer in. The loud metallic crash was very satisfying.

"Not happy this morning?"

The mild inquiry came from the doorway to the executive office. It startled Tessa for a moment. She hadn't expected her boss to be in. The Japanese conference started today, and normally the executives of the company would be meeting in the boardroom before flying off in the company helicopters. She pasted an extra bright smile on her face and swung to greet him.

Jerry Fraine was a big man with the kind of looks that suggested a cuddly, comfortable bear. He had frizzy grey-brown hair that stood out like a halo and a plump genial face that invited friendly confidences. He also had a razor-sharp mind, which could negotiate around the trickiest deals and land them. This made him the envy of the other ambitious executives of Callagan, Morris and Allen. All of whom had one ultimate ambition: to impress the managing director, Mr. Blaize Callagan.

Tessa liked being Jerry Fraine's secretary. He was appreciative of her skills, he was kind and considerate, and he had a dry sense of humour that made working with him a pleasure. He didn't try to lord it over her, and most importantly, he was happily married and not the least bit addicted to any playful slap-and-tickle around the office, thank heaven! It made for an easy relaxed atmosphere between them.

Tessa took a deep breath. "Never been happier," she tripped out airily. "Overflowing with buoyant spirits. God's in His heaven and all's right with the world." But if there was any justice, a bolt of lightning should hit Grant Durham right where it would hurt most!

Jerry grinned at the flaring glitter in her tawny gold eyes. The tigress in her was certainly running rampant today. Good, he thought. That should liven up proceedings. Perhaps it might even draw a little blood from Mr. Blaize Almighty Callagan. Although Jerry was careful not to let that thought show.

Tessa Stockton might be pocket-sized, but she was feisty, high-spirited and in Jerry's mind, utterly de--

lightful. A lovely woman. A real thoroughbred. Whose sharp wit was an amusing bonus to her sharp efficiency.

He observed, in secret amusement, that she was in a force-ten hurricane over something. Her long glossy brown hair was pulled tightly into a ponytail, a sure sign of furious impatience. Her tip-tilted nose was scenting battle. Her very sweetly curved mouth was stretched thin over a row of small white teeth that looked ready to bite. The delicate pointedness of her chin was decidedly thrust forward in a most aggressive manner this morning. Her long neck was stretched taut. Her exquisitely feminine body was quivering with tension.

"A slight twang of prewedding nerves?" he teased.

"The wedding," Tessa said through her teeth, "is off. O-F-F off!"

Jerry's eyebrows rose above his gold-rimmed spectacles. His mouth pursed. "It's quite normal, you know. Little tiffs do happen in the final rundown to the marriage ceremony."

Tessa's heart cramped. Infidelity was not a little tiff! It was on the tip of her tongue to say exactly that but she bit the words back at the last moment and clamped her mouth shut.

No need to say anything. No need to go public yet. No need to castigate Grant Durham for what he had done. Although he certainly deserved every bit of castigation he could get. To Tessa's mind, castration was probably better than castigation!

The humiliation searing her soul was too painful to discuss with anyone. She hadn't even told her sister when she had taken refuge there last night.

"Perhaps a little separation will help cool things down," Jerry went on smoothly.

Tessa gave him a blast with her eyes. The thick dark fringe of her eyelashes did nothing to fan the heat of molten gold.

Contrary to his own expectations, Jerry Fraine was not fried on the spot. He did a hasty reappraisal. He didn't relate to anger, and he liked to run a smooth ship. What employees did away from work was none of his business, and right now he had a problem. Which had to be addressed without further delay.

He relaxed, projected geniality, a soothing composure. "We have an emergency situation, Tessa."

She paused in midstep between the filing cabinet and her desk. She looked at him, really looked at him for the first time this morning. When Jerry Fraine put on that bland face and used that quiet voice, Tessa knew it was serious business. Her mind instantly changed gears; anger pushed out, concentration forced in.

Knowing that he now had her full attention, Jerry went on. "You're needed for the Japanese conference. Today. Right now, in fact."

Tessa was dumbstruck. "Why?" she croaked, unable to comprehend what was happening.

"Rosemary Davies was involved in a car accident on her way in this morning. She's in hospital. Nothing too serious but..."

Rosemary Davies, the ultra-cool, immaculately groomed, beautiful blonde, who was personal secretary to Blaize Callagan!

"I've chosen you to replace her."

Tessa's jaw dropped open. In her world, this was like trying to fly, then suddenly soaring to the sun. Jerry Fraine was an important man. Tessa thought she had reached her career heights when she was seconded to him. But Blaize Callagan—he was the absolute top! Only rarely did she see him, tall, powerful, riveting, a man who stood out amongst other men.

"You're free to be away for the three days of the conference, aren't you?"

Tessa unlocked her jaw. "Yes. Yes, I'm free." Very definitely free, her mind added savagely. Her Ex-fiancé had no further say in her life.

"Take a taxi home," Jerry instructed. "Pack fast and be back here in Blaize Callagan's office at ten-thirty. Not a second later."

Tessa jerked into action, wheeling around to shove the folder of reports into the filing cabinet and lock the drawer. Her mind was in a fever. She was going to fill in for Blaize Callagan's secretary. She would be in close contact with *him* for three whole days. Lord above! Her knees went weak even thinking about it. It would be a miracle if she didn't melt into a heap at his feet. If ever there was a man made for female fantasies, Blaize Callagan was *it!*

"And, Tessa . . ."

"Yes?" She tore the key out of the drawer and swung around, still dazed by the prospect ahead of her. "Yes, Jerry?"

"Please don't stuff up." He lifted his hands in imploring appeal. "I *am* a married man. I *do* have children to support."

"Well?" said Tessa, trying to get the point.

"I don't want Blaize Callagan to think I can't choose an efficient secretary."

Tessa pulled herself together. Forget the fantasies. This was business. Big Business, with capital *B*s. Blaize Callagan might be lethally attractive, but he was way out of her league, and all he wanted from her was her secretarial skills. If she acted like a star-struck idiot and messed up, it would reflect badly on Jerry Fraine. Not to mention the fact that it wouldn't do her own career any good, either. Since marriage was no longer on her immediate horizon, her career was all the more important to her, and she had better concentrate pretty fiercely on it.

"I'll do my best," she promised grimly.

"Better get moving then," Jerry advised.

Tessa snatched her handbag from the bottom drawer of her desk and raced for the door. It was only when she was in the corridor she realised that she couldn't possibly go home to her apartment to pack the clothes she would need. If Grant was still there . . . If that big-boobed floozy was still there . . .

Revulsion cramped Tessa's stomach as rage billowed through her mind once more. How could he do it? With that overblown creature in *her* bed! Between *her* sheets! It was the absolute pits of crass insensitivity! Which just went to show what a low-down rotten louse he was underneath all his surface charm!

It made Tessa positively ill to think that if she hadn't come back from her parents' place a day early, she wouldn't have found out what she had almost married. All these years thinking he was the only man she wanted, and she had been over the moon with happiness when he had finally proposed marriage to her. Yet here it was, only seven weeks to the wedding, and he could do that! He might even be creep enough to think he had free slather in her apartment today, since her ultimatum had given him until this evening to be out.

In retrospect, that had been wrong. What she should have done, of course, was hurl him and his floozy out there and then! Stark naked into the street! Except Grant was stronger than she was. And she had been so shocked, so outraged, so upset, that she hadn't been able to think straight. She had hurled a barrage of missiles at them, then stormed out of the apartment, feeling it was too contaminated to stay there.

She couldn't face that again.

She just couldn't!

There was nothing for it but to buy some clothes. That boutique up the end of the road, Executive Class—she would go there. It would probably cost her the earth, but so what! She no longer had to pay for a wedding dress.

Tessa worked it all out as she rode the elevator to the ground floor. She had all her toilet things and makeup in her weekend bag. Enough underclothes for three days. She needed three outfits that would go with her black high heels and handbag. Certainly the skirt and top she was wearing at the moment did not rate as suitable wear for Blaize Callagan's secretary.

Her heart fluttered in nervous anticipation. Blaize Callagan! Good Lord! How was she going to live up to *his* expectations? Well, she just had to keep her head and give it the best try she could, she told herself sternly. Jerry was counting on a good performance from her. For her own self-respect she had to perform well. She needed to feel good about something!

Forty minutes later, Tessa walked into the CMA building, wearing a black linen suit that hugged her figure in streamlined class. It was teamed with a pin-tucked, high-collared blouse in fine white lawn. The outfit had cost her four hundred dollars but it made Tessa feel like a million dollars, so to her mind, it was worth every cent. As were the two three-hundred-dollar outfits in the shopping bag she carried.

There was something very uplifting about being sinfully extravagant. Freedom, she told herself. All the scrimping and saving she had done for a future with Grant Durham was a thing of the past. It was her money now, to do with as she liked. She was no longer accountable to anyone but herself! Perhaps she would blow the rest of her bank account on a trip somewhere.

Meanwhile, this conference trip was a real godsend. It got her out of the city, away from any contact with Grant, and no doubt Blaize Callagan would keep her so busy she wouldn't have much time to think depressing thoughts. She hoped Grant would do one decent thing and get out of her apartment before she got back. Her continued absence for three days ought to hammer that message home to him.

Tessa arrived in her office with twenty minutes still up her sleeve. She quickly repacked her weekend bag, putting the things she wouldn't need into the plastic shopping bag. She was cramming that into the bottom drawer of her desk when she noticed the vinyl pouch that contained her "professional" glasses.

There was nothing wrong with Tessa's eyes, but the glasses were sometimes useful in projecting an image. She had first bought them when she came to Callagan, Morris and Allen so that she could keep other men from bothering her while she concentrated on Grant Durham. What a mistake that had been! But the glasses did give her an aura of serious reserve, helped along by the thick tortoiseshell rims. She suddenly thought it might be a very good idea to wear them as Blaize Callagan's secretary.

Her hair needed attention, too. Tessa wound her ponytail into a neat topknot, which she fastened with hairpins from her toilet bag. Then she tried on the glasses and examined the effect in her little hand mirror. They certainly helped to make her look a bit older than her twenty-four years. Gave her a more serious, earnest look, particularly with her hair up instead of falling loose. No one looking at her now could possibly think she was anything but a career professional.

She checked her watch. Five minutes to go. She zipped up her bag and set off for the elevators again, satisfied that she looked every bit as elegantly professional as Rosemary Davies, even though she was considerably shorter and nowhere near as upper class. However, there was nothing she could do about that.

Tessa worked on her composure as she rode up to the twentieth floor where Blaize Callagan reigned in the managing director's suite. Cool, calm and collected, she recited, like a mantra that would soothe all manner of palpitations.

Unfortunately, it didn't really work. Not once she was ushered into Blaize Callagan's office and she came face to face with him. It ran through Tessa's mind that there wouldn't be a woman in the whole world that could stand in front of Blaize Callagan and not suffer at least some palpitations.

He rose from his desk as she entered, six feet of masculine virility that had lost nothing in thirty-six years of high-powered living. His physique alone had strong sex appeal, lean enough to lend him a lithe elegance in the superbly tailored suits he wore—charcoal grey today—yet with that hint of danger in the hard muscularity, which proclaimed him superbly fit and ready for any type of confrontation.

He had a hard, angular face, barely fleshed, yet there was an austere and compelling beauty in its strong bone structure. His skin colour was a natural golden tan, complementing thick black hair and eyes so dark they were almost black, as well.

Tessa had never seen such penetrating inescapable eyes on anyone. They gleamed with a diamond-hard intelligence that would not allow release until he willed it. The moment they locked onto hers, a weird feeling of vulnerability crawled down Tessa's spine. They gave nothing away, expressed nothing. They simply imparted his dominance.

"Miss Stockton."

A short nod of the head by way of acceptance, or approval, or acknowledgement. Tessa had no idea which. His voice had a velvet purr that raised goose bumps on her skin. Somehow she made her tongue work.

"Yes, sir" was all she managed. Even that was a pure act of will.

He gestured an invitation to a chair in front of his desk. "Good of you to oblige at such short notice," he said pleasantly, then waited for her to sit down.

His eyes flicked over her in quick appraisal as she walked forward. Tessa had the nerve-quivering impression that nothing about her—absolutely nothing—escaped his notice. She almost slumped into the chair. Her legs were proving unreliable under pressure.

She forced herself to look at him inquiringly. His mouth moved into a little quirk that suggested some sensual satisfaction. His eyes stabbed briefly into hers, then he sat down and concentrated all his attention on the documents spread across his desk.

Tessa stared at him, waiting for him to give her instructions. She waited so long that her mind started to drift through all she knew about him. He was now a widower, but his wife, Candice, had been a famous model turned fashion designer. Her wild mane of red-gold curls had been her trademark, along with flashing green eyes, pearly skin and a tall, fabulous figure. An eminently suitable match for a man such as Blaize Callagan.

No doubt he was finding it difficult to replace her since her tragic death three years ago in a speedboat collision. But it wasn't for want of trying, according to the gossip that circulated about his affairs. Although whether or not the rumours were correct that he was bedding women right, left and centre, nothing—but absolutely nothing—distracted him from getting on with his business.

Everyone said he had a brilliant incisive mind, and certainly he couldn't operate an international company with such success if he wasn't shrewd at top-level decision-making. Tessa knew that it was Blaize Callagan who set all policies for CMA and saw that they were carried through, come hell or high water. Ruthless, he was, in getting his way. So it was rumoured. And reported by Jerry Fraine.

His head lifted.

Tessa snapped her mind to attention.

But his eyes didn't lift to hers. They seemed to study her legs, running a slow and very deliberate survey from the shape of her thighs—outlined by the narrow black skirt—to her knees, to her calves and ankles. He gave such concentrated attention to every detail that Tessa felt every bone and muscle had been mapped and committed to memory. The expression on his face said he liked the map. Very much. He gave a quick, short, decisive nod of his head, then pulled his gaze to the documents again.

He must have been thinking of something, Tessa reasoned, although it didn't make her feel less conscious of the prickling of her skin against her stockings. And when, a couple of minutes later, he stared at her breasts, which her suit jacket moulded to prominent effect, no reasoning Tessa could come up with stopped her nipples from doing what they shouldn't. He seemed to know, to place them exactly. Those X-ray eyes of his were very, very unsettling. She was intensely relieved when he gave another nod and they dropped to the documents again.

Tessa checked her watch. She had been here fifteen minutes. It seemed ridiculous that he didn't ask her to do something. Why had he demanded that she be in his office at ten-thirty if he didn't want to put her to work? Did he think she would be incompetent? That she couldn't possibly measure up to the perfect Rosemary?

Tessa's professional pride stirred. She was as good a secretary as anybody, and could run rings around most. It was an insult to leave her sitting like this. An insult to Jerry, as well. She couldn't let it go on. In fact, she wasn't sure that the way he had studied her legs and breasts in that disassociated manner wasn't an even worse insult. Blaize Callagan might be the big boss, but she *was* a fellow human being. And a damned good secretary!

Tessa worked some moisture into her mouth and mentally adopted a brisk professional manner. "Where do you want me to start, sir?" she asked.

"At the beginning," he muttered, without looking up.

A blaze of resentment glittered in her tawny gold eyes. Pride puffed through her mind. He wasn't going to patronise her as though she were some silly dumb cluck! She dragged in a deep breath and spoke with very cool precision.

"If you would be kind enough to spell out specifically what you want . . ."

Finally the dark eyes shot up and fastened on hers. "The usual," he said, "although everything will be happening much faster, I expect, than what you are normally used to. Although the sessions will be taped for future reference, you will take a note of everything that is said, not only as a check to the tapes but also for my easy reference. After the meetings, you will be required to word-process any memos, directives or queries. You will liaise with your opposite number. You will make sure that everyone has what they need. Apart from that, every important thing is to be reduced to writing," he said in rapid-fire delivery. "With exactness and precision. Can you manage that?"

"Yes, sir," she fired back.

"And, Miss Stockton . . ."

"Yes, sir?"

"There is nearly a hundred million dollars of joint project money at stake."

"Yes, sir."

"Please . . . try not to stuff up, Miss Stockton."

"Yes, sir."

"Everything that you do will be important, Miss Stockton. Please appreciate that."

"Yes, sir."

His eyes returned to his documents.

Tessa felt she'd just been put through the wringer—picked up, squeezed dry, then hung out on a waiting line again.

"And is there anything you want me to do immediately, sir?" she grated, determined to prove that she wasn't the ninny he took her for.

He looked up, and this time he really looked at her, his eyes gathering a speculative interest as he examined hers. After several heart-stopping moments, he softly said, "I don't think you'd be able to oblige."

Tessa flushed at his mortifying judgement of her.

A gleam of some secret inner amusement danced into the dark eyes, and again his mouth moved into a sensual little quirk. "Perhaps some other time."

Tessa didn't know how to interpret that. But his private amusement was not at all mollifying to her injured pride.

"The Japanese delegation has been held up for an hour or so. That's the reason for the delay," he said more briskly. "In the meantime, arm yourself with your tools of trade, Miss Stockton. Rosemary left an attaché case full of documents and documentation on her desk if you would like to check through them. Anything you might think you need, you will find in her office. Through the door behind you," he directed.

Tessa almost leapt from her chair, eager to do something useful.

"And, Miss Stockton..."

"Yes, sir?"

"In this business, it is impossible to anticipate everything. If there is anything we need at any time, you have my authority behind you all the way. Over everyone."

"Thank you, sir," Tessa said in some dismay. She found absolute power a scary concept. The responsibility of it was positively frightening. But she reassured herself with the thought that Blaize Callagan had accepted the responsibility of backing her. Although if she stuffed up...

"Some problem, Miss Stockton?" he inquired, as she stood there furiously thinking.

"No, sir." She was *not* going to stuff up. "Thank you, sir," she added for good measure, then turned briskly towards the door he had indicated.

However, as she walked across the room to his secretary's adjoining office, she had the very strong sensation that Blaize Callagan's penetrating dark eyes were studying her bottom and every movement it made. No doubt it amused him.

Never in her life had Tessa felt more conscious of being a woman, or more conscious of a man being a man. The tension that tightened her nerves had nothing whatsoever to do with proving her competence as a secretary. It was the way Blaize Callagan kept looking at her!

CHAPTER TWO

AT PRECISELY eleven-thirty, Blaize Callagan collected Tessa from his secretary's office. They were driven to the helicopter in a stretch limousine. He read documents all the way.

Her awareness of him would lessen, Tessa told herself. However, she couldn't help noticing that his fingers were long and supple. Occasionally he rubbed his thumb over their inner pads as his hand was poised ready to turn another page. The soft tactile movement was somehow disturbing. So was the tangy scent of his after-shave lotion in the close confinement of the car.

He said nothing to her and Tessa felt constrained not to break his concentration. Once the conference started she would be busy enough, she decided, so she might as well relax while she could. Except that was proving utterly impossible.

The fine woollen fabric of his trousers was stretched tightly across his thighs. She wondered if he worked out at a gym. Powerful muscles weren't formed and maintained without some kind of exercise. Tessa knew that from her aerobics class. On the other hand, Blaize Callagan might get all the exercise he needed elsewhere. Although Grant—the two-timing fink—didn't have hard muscular thighs like that, so perhaps Blaize Callagan did work out at a gym.

Three other executives were standing by the helicopter when they arrived. One of them was Jerry Fraine. He stared at Tessa, his eyebrows shot up, his mouth twitched, he passed a hand across his face, then he quickly swung toward the helicopter. His big burly shoulders visibly shook.

Whether it was a result of prolonged nervous tension, Tessa didn't know, but she had to swallow an impetuous giggle herself. Jerry had never seen her look so prim and proper and professional. And the glasses, of course, had been a joke between them. She hoped, when he recovered his composure, he would appreciate the effort she had made on behalf of her image. After all, it was for Jerry Fraine's benefit as well as her own. Not that it seemed to be working very effectively. So far Blaize Callagan didn't seem to see her as a career professional. Only as a body. A female body.

The conference was being held at Peppers, a highly reputable country hotel in the Hunter River Valley. It was set among the famous vineyards that produced some of the best Australian wines. Although it was about two hundred kilometres from Sydney by road, it was little more than a twenty-minute flight by helicopter.

Tessa had never been to Peppers, and she had never been in a helicopter, either. As soon as she saw the executives climbing aboard, she knew she had a problem. No way in the world was she going to be able to take the high step into the cabin in her narrow skirt. She heaved a deep sigh and looked at Blaize Callagan. He met her glance with a wickedly knowing gleam in his dark eyes.

"I'll lift you," he said.

Tessa burned. "Thank you," she bit out.

The pilot had already taken their attaché cases from them to stow in the baggage area. Tessa expected Blaize Callagan to hoist her up from her waist. He didn't. Before she even approached the step to the cabin, he swooped and lifted her right off her feet and into his arms.

"Nice body weight, Miss Stockton," he remarked appreciatively.

"Thank you, sir," Tessa whispered as she tried to recapture her breath.

One arm was around her thighs. His other arm was around her shoulders, with a hand coming perilously close to curling under her arm to the outside swell of her breast. She was pressed against a broad and unrelenting chest.

"Look after yourself, do you, Stockton?"

She looked him straight in the eye, blazing gold meeting devilish black. "I try to keep in trim."

"Good work, Stockton. Try to keep it that way."

"Oh, I will, sir. I will."

His mouth wore that funny quirk as he carried her forward and lifted her into her cabin seat with all the ease in the world. He really had very sensual lips. Tessa felt he knew just what to do with them and used them accordingly. To taunt, tease, excite or provoke. Right at this moment, she felt very provoked. And teased. And taunted. And if she was totally honest with herself, treacherously excited. He certainly was a very strong man.

He released her smoothly, without the slightest suggestion of taking any liberties, and Tessa was left wondering if he was playing games with her or not. She concentrated on fastening her seat belt until he was settled in the seat in front of her, next to the pilot. She wished she had bought a pantsuit. She was almost sure he had enjoyed touching her like that.

The helicopter lifted off. When the heat in her cheeks became slightly less painful, Tessa turned to look at Jerry, who was sitting next to her. Impossible to talk, but she would have liked a look of moral support from him. He had his gold-rimmed spectacles off. One hand was lifted to his eyes, finger and thumb squeezing the eyelids hard. His brow was furrowed. His head was bent. He looked as if he was fiercely concentrated in prayer... or something.

Tessa sighed. No help there. Maybe Jerry hated flying. Or maybe he was praying that she wouldn't stuff up. She beamed a hard thought at the back of Blaize Callagan's head. I am not here for your amusement, Blaize Callagan, she told him. And my body—fit or not—is no business of yours. You either take me seriously, or don't take me at all!

Except she was here in this helicopter, and on her way with him, and she couldn't exactly jump off in midair. In fact, there was very little she could do about it, so she turned her head to the view below and watched the city give way to country. At least she was getting away from other problems for a while.

There had to be someone down there, she thought. Someone a whole lot better than Grant Durham. Someone who would at least be faithful to the so-called love he talked about. Tessa wondered if Blaize Callagan had been faithful to his wife. Maybe men weren't faithful animals. But she certainly wasn't going to marry one who couldn't be faithful to her seven weeks before their wedding day!

Tessa heaved another sigh. How was she going to tell her mother the wedding was off? She could readily imagine the hysterics and the recriminations. "What will people think?" and, "All the arrangements are made!" and, "You've been wanting to marry Grant for four years, Tessa! You won't get anyone if you don't have him." Her mother was going to throw an absolute fit. Reason would have nothing to do with it.

At least her father would listen. He had never been all that keen on Grant. Besides, her father was about to be saved a lot of money on the wedding reception. He would appreciate that more than her mother did. Tessa had always found her father a sane, sensible man.

It seemed no time at all before they were over the Hunter River Valley. The rolling hills were lined with rows and rows of grapevines. The helicopter swooped in towards an impressive complex of colonial-styled buildings situated on the top of a small hill. Cream walls, green roof and verandahs all around. Nothing higher than two storeys. Landscaped gardens close in, and expanses of lawn rolling down the hill with lovely stands of native gum trees and a huge lake-like dam to add interest.

They landed on the lawn near the tennis court. Blaize Callagan lifted Tessa out of the helicopter as efficiently as he had lifted her into it. Apparently they were the last to arrive. The verandah above the slope of lawn was crowded with company people and a smattering of Japanese, all enjoying a preluncheon drink while they waited for the big guns to lead proceedings.

Tessa looked at the grassed slope to be traversed and regretted her spindly high heels. Blaize Callagan offered his arm.

"Please try not to fall flat on your face, Stockton. It wouldn't create a good impression," he murmured out of the corner of his mouth.

"I'll hang onto you like grim death, sir," she retorted.

"A lively way to meet your end, Stockton," he said with a totally impassive countenance. "Might I suggest a more forward pressure on your toes?"

"At your command, sir."

"Nice attitude, Stockton."

"Thank you, sir."

She made it up to the verandah without mishap. At which point, she became nothing but a cipher at Blaize Callagan's side until luncheon was over, although she was treated with impeccable courtesy by all the men present, Australian and Japanese. Her opposite number, with whom she would have to liaise, was a man. Who, she was pleased to note, was as short as she was, which made him a whole lot less intimidating than he might have been. She was the only woman from either side.

At two o'clock, they all trooped down to the conference centre and the nitty-gritty business began. Tessa had no time to admire the facilities provided, the fine proportions of the big conference room, the interesting paintings on the walls or the artistic floral arrangements. She concentrated hard on her shorthand notes, arranging them in a system for easy reference points—the names of the speakers, their contributions to the discussion, the proposals, the objections, the suggested compromises.

Jerry Fraine was good. She felt positively proud of her boss's negotiating skills. But Blaize Callagan was the pivot, without a doubt. Everything turned around him. It was an education to listen and watch as he swung an argument or worked around it, seizing advantages, defusing problems, plotting a winning course.

They broke briefly for afternoon tea, which was served in the reception room, allowing people to mill around and relax for a breathing space.

"Got all that, Stockton?" Blaize asked as he accompanied her out of the conference room.

"Yes, sir," she replied confidently.

"I hope so, Stockton. This is one tough nut to crack and I'm going to need every last bit of ammunition we can get," he said grimly.

Tessa held her tongue. She thought he had been doing extremely well. The majority of Japanese seemed to be in agreement with what he was pushing. Nevertheless, he obviously knew his business better than she did. When they returned for the last session of the day, Tessa made sure she didn't miss a beat. If any little thing was critical, she had it faithfully recorded.

At five o'clock they broke for the day. But it was far from the end of her working day. A hotel staff member was on hand to lead Blaize Callagan to his accommodation, and Tessa was taken along with him. They were led away from the main buildings of the hotel complex to a private cottage on the edge of the grounds.

A verandah led into a large living room. Office equipment had been set up for them here; a worktable holding an IBM computer and a laser printer with a pile of stationery for ready use. A marvellous fireplace opened to both the living room and the dining room. There was a well-equipped kitchen and four bedrooms. But only *one* bathroom. To be shared by the occupants. The staff member showed them through every room, pointing out all the facilities and assuring Blaize Callagan that anything he wanted, anything at all, was on call.

Tessa noticed that her suitcase had been put in one of the bedrooms. It had obviously been arranged that she was staying here, with *him*, alone with him!

She tried telling herself that this was where it had been planned for Rosemary Davies to stay, but it didn't help to calm her pulse. The truth of the matter was she didn't know if Blaize Callagan's relationship with Rosemary Davies was purely professional. She had never heard any rumours to the contrary, but this was certainly a more intimate arrangement than she had figured on. It was bad enough having to share a bathroom with him. How was she going to sleep tonight? Wasn't this situation at the very least compromising?

On the other hand, it was common practice these days for people of the opposite sex to share houses or apartments in the high rental climate of Sydney. Lots of women felt safer with a guy in residence. No one raised eyebrows at it any more, or jumped to the conclusion that sharing accommodation meant sharing beds.

Tessa worked hard at assuring herself that her reputation was not about to be shot to pieces by staying under the same roof as Blaize Callagan. After all, this was part of the hotel and they did have separate bedrooms. Making any objection to the arrangement was completely out of the question.

But the moment the hotel staff member walked out the door and left her alone with Blaize Callagan in the living room, all the sane and sensible reasoning in the world could not dispel the feeling of danger—in capital letters.

"A ten-minute break for you to unpack or wash or whatever, Stockton," Blaize Callagan instructed. "Then I want transcripts of everything said by the Japanese speakers."

Tessa breathed a small sigh of relief. She could handle work. "Yes, sir."

"What would you like to drink?"

"Coffee, sir."

"White and one sugar, wasn't it?"

"Yes, sir."

She was surprised that he remembered such a trivial detail from the coffee she had had at lunch. It reminded her of a few other things he might have memorised about her, and she felt a surge of heat tingling outwards towards her skin. She turned away and headed for her bedroom fast before the blush became too obvious.

She even felt self-conscious about using the toilet with *him* wandering around nearby. Which was absolutely ridiculous! She ran cold water over her wrists for a few seconds, then dabbed it over her hot face. Stay cool, calm and collected, she fiercely instructed herself.

He might be the sexiest-looking man she had ever seen, but that didn't mean he found her sexy. Although he had taken an inordinate interest in her body. Nevertheless, he knew as well as she did that she was out of his class, and this accommodation had obviously been arranged for his convenience in a strictly business sense. He wanted her for work. That's all. And she had to oblige him as best she could.

Unpacking didn't take long. She hung up her new dresses, although both of them were in uncrushable fabrics, then set out her toilet things in the bathroom. She checked her appearance in the mirror—still tidy—then returned to the living room to work.

Blaize Callagan was stretched out in an armchair, suit coat off, tie loosened, top two buttons of his shirt undone. He was nursing a drink in his hand, something with ice, and he looked very relaxed. It did not make Tessa feel relaxed at all. It made her a lot more conscious of his body.

"Coffee by the computer," he said.

"Thank you, sir."

The computer and printer were already switched on, ready to go. Tessa opened her attaché case, which had been placed on the table beside them, removed her notebook and sat down. She sipped the coffee as she ran her fingers over the keyboard, setting up the word-processing program to suit her needs.

"Kick your shoes off, if you like, Stockton. Undo your jacket. Be comfortable."

"I'm comfortable as I am, thank you, sir," she said, keeping her eyes glued to the monitor screen. It was bad enough having him flaunting his body at her. She wasn't about to let her guard down.

"Put each speaker on separate pages and pass them to me as they're done," he instructed.

"Yes, sir."

Tessa worked at top speed for the next hour, transcribing her shorthand into neat sheets of printing. She did not pass them to Blaize Callagan. He was up and waiting for each sheet to emerge from the printer, taking it away, studying it, pacing around, pouncing on the next one, occasionally muttering to himself.

"What next, sir?" Tessa asked, when she had finished the last Japanese speaker.

He looked up from the page he had just snatched, frowned at her. "I've got to think. Go and have a bath or something, Stockton." He checked his watch. "Predinner drinks in the bar at seven. Be ready."

"Yes, sir."

"There'll be no business over dinner. The Japanese don't work that way. So you can relax for a while, Stockton."

"Yes, sir. Thank you, sir."

She was already dismissed, his concentration back on the pages in his hand.

The way he could switch on and off was little short of incredible, Tessa thought, as the evening progressed. He was tense and silent, inwardly focused, until they reached the bar in the main building. In an instant he was emanating goodwill and fellowship. Over dinner he was a charming host, telling jokes, swapping stories, affable and interesting, controlling the conversation with enviable ease and mastery. The moment they walked out of the hotel, he closed into himself again, tense and silent.

They were halfway back to the cottage before he spoke, and that was only to use Tessa as a sounding board for his thoughts.

"We've got a real problem. The way things are shaping up, I can't see the Japanese getting *ringi,*" he said abruptly.

"What's *ringi,* sir?" Tessa asked. She had never heard the term before.

"Their seal of approval. Every delegate has to give it before the project can go ahead. It's a symbol of their complete dedication and commitment to the project. A totally different system to ours. I can make a unilateral decision and force it through. Saves a lot of time and trouble. But they won't move without consensus."

The impatience and frustration in his voice told Tessa what he thought about *that* system. But then Blaize Callagan was obviously a born dictator. Tessa thought the *ringi* system was a lot fairer than orders from on high. Less open to abuse. But she kept her opinion to herself.

"Stockton, what happens when you run into an immovable object at full speed?"

"You get hurt, sir."

"Don't be a fool, Stockton. I'm talking about me."

This left Tessa feeling confused. Did Blaize Callagan think he was invulnerable to hurt? Was he? "I don't know, sir," she said. It seemed the safest comment.

"There are only two things to do, Stockton. Run into it and get hurt, as you suggest. No point in trying to shift it. That's impossible. The far better thing is—get around it."

"Yes, sir."

"I'm going to sidestep *ringi,* " he said decisively.

"Yes, sir."

By this time they were walking up the steps to the cottage.

"Need to write a memo, Stockton."

"Yes, sir."

As soon as they entered the living room, Tessa went straight to the computer, switched it on and sat down, readying herself for his dictation. He paced up and down the room, gathering his thoughts.

His suit coat came off. It was tossed onto a chair. His tie made its exit, as well. Four buttons on his shirt were flicked open, revealing a dark sprinkle of hair below his throat. Tessa was beginning to feel a bit tight around the throat herself.

He paused, frowned, then started to dictate, setting out the strategy he had decided upon in clear precise terms. Tessa's fingers flew to keep up with him. There was another long pause for more concentration. He removed his cuff links and rolled his shirt sleeves up to his elbows. His forearms were indeed muscular. Tessa hoped the undressing was going to stop there. It was getting very, very distracting.

"There's a lot of nervous tension here, Stockton," he remarked.

"I've noticed that, sir."

The dark eyes stabbed at her with amused appreciation. "I'm glad you have more words in your vocabulary than 'yes, sir,' Stockton. It comes as a relief."

"Yes, sir."

He dictated further points for the memo then came to stand behind her chair to read the monitor screen. "Turn it back to the beginning, Stockton," he directed.

"Would you like me to print it out, sir?"

"No. Just roll it through the monitor for me. I'll tell you what to add or delete as we go."

"Yes, sir."

How Tessa held her concentration together she didn't know. Several times he leaned over her to point out a place in the printing on the screen, thrusting his bare forearm right in front of her eyes, making her overwhelmingly aware of male flesh and muscle...and the long supple fingers...and the warmth of his breath near her ear...and the scent of his strong masculinity.

Several times her fingers fumbled and she had to correct her mistakes. He made no critical comment. He patiently waited until she was ready to go on. At last they came to the end of it. Then he asked her to turn it to the beginning and roll it through again.

"Very tense, Stockton," he commented. "I think we should do something about it."

Tessa had no suggestions. She didn't know if he was commenting on her or him or the memo. She couldn't even bring herself to say, "Yes, sir." She sat there in piano-wire tautness, waiting for his next instruction, hoping she could carry it out with some air of competence.

She felt a hairpin being drawn out of her topknot. Then another one. And another one. She stopped breathing. Her heart slammed around her chest. After several moments of blank shock—and the loss of several more hairpins—Tessa's mind dictated that she should start breathing again because her chest was getting very constricted and her heart was protesting quite painfully. Her mind added that she ought to say something, as well. But before she could find some appropriate words, he spoke.

"Nice hair, Stockton," he said as her ponytail fell down and his fingers drifted through the silky weight of the thick tresses. He leaned over her shoulder and placed a bundle of hairpins on the table. Then he went to work on the rubber band, gently untwining it to release her ponytail. "You'll feel a lot better with your hair down," he said.

"Mr. Callagan..." Tessa almost choked on his name. She decided it was best not to make an issue of her hair at this late point, but to get his mind—and hers—firmly directed onto business. "Would you like this memo printed out now?"

"No."

The rubber band was tossed on top of the pins. His fingers lifted her hair away from its former constraint, fanning the long tresses out in all their glossy glory before sliding through them to gently massage her scalp.

"Do you want to make more changes to the memo?" she asked, beginning to feel quite desperate about his absorption with her hair.

"Perhaps later. Needs thinking about. Feeling less tense now?"

"Yes. Thank you." It was a terrible lie, but what else could she say?

"A pleasure, Stockton," he purred in his velvet tone. And thankfully removed his hands from her hair. Then, just as she sucked in a much-needed scoop of oxygen, he said, "Let me help you off with your jacket." And he was bending over her again, his hands working on the buttons at her waist with swift effectiveness.

She froze. Her mind went into stasis for the few critical seconds that it took for him to have her jacket unbuttoned and opened wide.

"Just lean forward a bit and I'll slide it off your shoulders," he said.

Tessa's mind burst out of stasis and into frantic activity. It was only her jacket. He hadn't groped over her breasts or anything. She leaned forward and lifted her arms out of the sleeves as he smoothly pulled the jacket away from her.

"Smart suit, Stockton," he said, as he tossed the top half of it on a chair. "Does you credit."

"Thank you, sir," Tessa managed to croak.

Somehow, his approval of her choice of clothes didn't carry much weight at this moment. Some belated instinct of self-preservation urged her to stop sitting like a waiting dummy and take some positive initiative. She stood up and turned to face him. It wasn't easy meeting his eyes. First she had to drag her own up from his chest—there were more of his shirt buttons undone. Right to the waist!

"I think," she forced out, "since you don't need me..."

"Oh, but I do need you, Stockton," he said softly, the dark eyes locking onto hers in hot, purposeful intent. "I need you very much."

He moved. One hand slid around her waist, the other gently tilted her chin, keeping her eyes fastened to his as he drew her lower body against his, letting her know the shape and urgency of what he desired of her. "Very much," he repeated with slow deliberate emphasis.

CHAPTER THREE

THERE WAS ABSOLUTELY nothing unmistakable about what was going on now. The hardness pressing into her stomach had a rampant virility that left Tessa in no doubt whatsoever. Her mind was suddenly very clear, even though the rest of her was a melting mess.

In the clarity of her mind was one brightly burning thought: Blaize Callagan found her desirable. Urgently desirable. Her erstwhile fiancé had fancied someone else, but Blaize Callagan—this man amongst men—fancied *her!*

All the same, that sweet balm to her wounded soul was no reason to lose her head over him, Tessa swiftly reasoned. Her hands fluttered up to his chest. As a means of protest they were hopelessly ineffectual. One of her thumbs hit bare warm flesh and stuck there. She cleared her throat.

"I think..."

"Stockton, this is not the time for thinking," he advised kindly. He lifted his hand from her chin, took off her glasses and lobbed them onto the table behind her. His hand moved to her throat and began unbuttoning her blouse.

"Interesting thing about your eyes, Stockton," he said, looking into them with mesmerising intensity. "They don't look at all weak or vacant without your glasses on. In fact, they appear brighter . . . and infinitely more fascinating."

"Thank you, sir," Tessa said, swallowing hard. "I'd like to say, sir, that this isn't a good idea." At least her voice could register a protest, even though the rest of her was playing traitor to any sense of right or propriety.

"On the contrary, Stockton. It's the best release for tension I know. I've had a lot of experience."

"Yes, sir. I'm sure you have, sir." He was unbuttoning her blouse with such swift and smooth expertise that the buttons seemed to know they had to obey him without falter. "But it so happens, sir, that I don't go in for one-night stands."

"Perish the thought, Stockton. We have at least two nights."

Tessa took a deep breath, trying desperately to ignore what he was doing and act with as much dignity as she could. "Look, sir, just because your normal secretary performs this service for you, doesn't mean you can expect . . ."

"Stockton." He looked at her severely as his hand continued its unrelenting intent, parting her blouse and tracing soft sensual paths across the swell of her breasts with gentle fingertips. "I do not require or want this service—as you put it—from Rosemary Davies. I make it a practice of never mixing business with pleasure. It's a ruinous mistake."

Her skin trembled with excitement under his touch. "Then why are you doing it?" she argued with impeccable logic.

"One must adapt to extraordinary circumstances," he replied with commanding authority.

Extraordinary... The word spun around Tessa's mind, gathering a hypnotic power. It certainly fitted this situation. He was right about that. It was extraordinary that Blaize Callagan should *desire* her, and extraordinary that she was actually letting him take such liberties. Not only letting him, but liking what he was doing to her. I need to feel desired, she thought. And he was not just anybody! In the normal course of events, she would never again be with Blaize Callagan like this. It was time out of time. Extraordinary circumstances. An encounter. For both of them.

Whether he took her silence as encouragement or assent, Tessa didn't know. Perhaps he saw the softening of vulnerability in her eyes, or was hell-bent on pressing his own will anyway. Whatever...

He found the front fastening of her bra and undid it without the slightest fumble or difficulty. Very softly, he grazed his fingers under the nylon lace, gradually peeling it away and replacing its cup with the warm palm of his hand. With exquisite delicacy his thumb began a sweeping caress over her breast. Not once did he glance down to look at the flesh he had bared, or see what he was doing. His eyes never left hers.

She didn't look down, either. She stared at him, her mind achurn with alien thoughts, but she was conscious of her body responding to his touch with wild spasms of nervous excitement.

Why not, she argued feverishly. The only man she had ever given herself to had been unfaithful to her last night. Why shouldn't she have this man? Why shouldn't she have this experience? Grant certainly hadn't nursed any scruples about sampling what he wanted. She was free to do anything she liked. With whomever she liked. And right now she was being offered the kind of fantasy that Blaize Callagan had always evoked. It would never come her way again. So why not grab it while she could? Wouldn't she regret it afterwards if she didn't?

"Don't be inflexible, Stockton. It's ruined more people than I care to name," Blaize said persuasively. "What we have here is an intensely desirable situation. And to be perfectly frank, there is a great deal of tension between us. Much more tension than can be summarily dismissed. Don't you agree?"

Desirable, desirable... The word beat around Tessa's brain, heightening the temptation. Where had all her fine standards of morality got her? Out in the cold while a big-boobed floozy took over her bed. Well, she needn't be cold tonight! Blaize Callagan wanted her. And, yes... she wanted to know what he was like as a lover, however brief the encounter.

"Agreed," she said, in a rush of heady recklessness.

"No regrets?" he asked.

If she had any regrets afterwards... well, she would live with them. At least they would make better memories than seeing Grant and that creature in her bed.

"No regrets," she said.

She felt the rise of his chest at his sharp intake of breath. His eyes were instantly hooded, but not before Tessa saw the flaring glitter of triumph in them. He had got his way, she thought, with ruthless disregard for anything but his own desire. Yet she didn't resent it. He had at least asked her, although he had certainly loaded the dice before rolling out that little nicety.

Perhaps it was that quality in him that made him so provocative, so exciting. The will to dare, to take the opportunity, to win. And the arrogance of the mind behind that will.

But she also had a will, and Tessa knew inside herself that she was not his conquest. She had made a choice, for better or for worse. And she did not intend to be a passive victim to his will.

She moved her hands, sliding them under his opened shirt. If she was going to do it, she might as well fulfil every fantasy she had ever had. No point in holding back.

He went completely still, perhaps surprised by her initiative, perhaps savouring her touch on his flesh. He was, Tessa thought, a very sensual man. He waited as she pulled his shirt apart, pushed it off his shoulders, but he didn't move his hold on her to let her drag it off his arms.

He was beautifully made, sleek and powerful, the muscles of his chest firmly delineated, his shoulders broad and strong, his upper arms... Tessa ran her fingernails down them, testing the tensile strength underneath his gleaming skin.

She heard his breath hiss through his teeth and looked at him through her thick lashes, the gleaming gold of her eyes smoky with a savage desire of her own. "Not all your own way, sir," she taunted softly.

He smiled, and it was the smile of a predator about to take up the hunt. He lifted his hand from her breast, slid it under her hair, caressed the nape of her neck, tilted her head back, then, holding her firmly, brought his lips down on hers.

He kissed her hungrily, with quick shifting pressures, sensuality mixed with an aggression that barely allowed her to catch breath. She reached up to wind her arms around his neck. He curled his hand under her bottom and hoisted her into more intimate contact with his aroused state, scraping the softness of her breasts up his chest, crushing her against him as he turned and headed for the closest bedroom.

Tessa's shoes slipped off her dangling feet. He kicked them aside. He laughed a deep throaty laugh as he stood her on the bed and swiftly disposed of her blouse and bra. "I knew you were beautiful," he said, and with his mouth he paid devastating homage to both her breasts as his hands worked to strip off her skirt.

It felt so good, so exultantly good that he didn't want her to have huge melons like that woman Grant had put in her bed. She moved herself with a fierce abandonment against his gloriously ravaging mouth, inviting, enticing, withdrawing, plunging forward, digging her fingers into his hair, making him work, shifting from one taut mound of pulsing flesh to the other, feeding a deep savage satisfaction that had very little to do with Blaize Callagan . . . except he was the perfect person to give her what she wanted.

Whether he sensed this or not, she didn't know. Suddenly he wrenched his head out of her grasp and lowered her down on the pillows. He pulled the rest of her clothes off her legs with swift efficiency but no delicacy at all. Tessa didn't care about that. She didn't care about anything except what might be coming next.

He was breathing hard, harder than she was. And there was a gleam of raw savagery about his face as he tore off his shirt and threw down his trousers. He was every bit as magnificent as she had imagined he would be. He sat beside her to remove his shoes and socks, and she ran her fingernails down his taut thigh. She had actually fancied doing that in the limousine this morning.

An animal growl rumbled from his throat. He twisted, caught her hands, pushed them above her head. Then with slow and very deliberate control he moved onto the bed, stretching out on his side next to her, leaning over her with dark simmering intent. *His way*... that was what was glittering in his eyes.

It stirred a strong ambivalence in Tessa, the desire to know his way and the desire to turn it into something different, unique both for him and herself. She did not want him to use her and forget her. Even though she could be nothing more than a memory to him in time to come, she wanted the memory to stick. As something special.

He held her hands inactive with one detaining arm so that he could use his free hand to touch her where he willed. He stroked her throat, the now wildly pulsating sensitivity of her breasts, her stomach, her thighs. He watched her face as her flesh quivered to his touch.

Tessa made no move, no sound. She watched him in silence, both loving and defying his sensual expertise. Take me when you want, but I'll take you, too, she promised him.

He bent and ran the tip of his tongue between her lips. She touched it with hers. He moved into a slow escalation of the kiss, teasing, tantalising, playing for maximum sensation. He slid his hand between her thighs, skilfully arousing her, slowly driving excitement and anticipation to breaking point.

She knew instinctively that it was what he wanted, to make her cry out, to plead, to make her want him beyond any thread of control. Every nerve end in her body screamed for release but she held on, grimly refusing to be easy for him.

She didn't know why it was so important to her. Maybe it was some dark deep unfathomable sense of revenge. The man she had loved had taken her for granted. Treated her with disrespect. Thought he could get away with anything. If ever there was an archetypal man, it was Blaize Callagan. And this time, this time with him, nothing about her was going to be taken for granted.

"Relax," he growled.

"Please let my hands go, sir."

He released a long shuddering sigh, which told her he was stretched fairly taut himself. "Try not to claw me to death, Stockton."

"It will only be a little blood, sir." A drop of life, that's all it would be, but he would share it with her. She would make him.

"Somehow I feel I can't count on that, Stockton."

He sensed the dark well of intensity in her, and it was getting to him. Tessa felt a thrill of power. "Trust me, sir."

"With those tigress eyes?"

She smiled. "He who rides a tiger takes his life in his own hands, sir." It was a challenge that a man such as Blaize Callagan would never back away from.

His eyes narrowed. "Very profound, Stockton."

"Thank you, sir."

He released her hands, then waited, tensely poised, to see what she would do with them. She curled one around his head and gently raked her fingers through his thick black hair, feeling the texture of it, enjoying its soft springiness. She lifted her other hand to his face, obeying an impulse to trace his beautiful bone structure with her fingertips; his brow, his cheeks, his nose, his jawline. It was a curiously exhilarating exploration, almost as though she was touching the inner man under his skin.

She wanted to touch his lips, the finer texture there, the sharp line of definition that outlined them. But he suddenly opened his mouth and sucked her fingers in, biting them a little before releasing them.

He bent and kissed her hard. She responded with a passion that fired even more passion from him. She ran her foot down his calf. He shuddered. She ran her fingernails down his back, very lightly, but he reared up, an inarticulate cry tearing from his throat.

He took her then, the need to smash her control so intense that his possession of her was explosive. Tessa's response was instant and aggressive, riding the storm of sensation with all the intoxicating elation of a surfer on a rip curl, balancing her body through every rhythmic change, every wild contortion, welding with him in a mad drive for more and more sensation that drove them both to excesses in their fierce desire to exhaust the other.

It ended in peaceful togetherness. She melted around him, he lost himself in her, and their sweat-slicked bodies slid finally to rest.

For a long time, neither moved. They were totally spent, floating mindlessly on a tide that had ebbed but still had them in its grip. Eventually Blaize summoned enough energy to lift himself away from her and roll onto his back. They lay side by side, not talking, not touching, not moving.

Tessa had no idea what he was thinking but the silence didn't worry her. She was busy with her own thoughts as she reviewed what had just happened with a sense of awe and wonder.

It had been a wild experience. In all her time with Grant, she had never been so . . . so— She searched for some way to express it, but there simply weren't words for what had happened with Blaize Callagan. Involved? Crazy? Uninhibited? Intensely focussed? She couldn't even call what they'd done together lovemaking.

It had nothing to do with love. They hardly knew each other. Yet it had certainly been more intimate than any lovemaking she had experienced with Grant. More physically intimate. It left her feeling she had never really known herself. In hindsight, she was shocked that she was capable of that act of sexual aggression and totally primitive gratification. It was a revelation. A new dimension to herself that she had never suspected.

Even more disturbing—all she had ever felt for Grant Durham seemed weak and insubstantial, as if he wasn't reality at all. Blaize Callagan, whom she had always thought of as a fantasy, was the raw reality. Which was very confusing.

She wasn't emotionally involved with Blaize Callagan. Except in a terribly mixed up way. He certainly affected her emotions, her body, her way of thinking, everything.

She didn't think she affected him in the same way. Obviously he had only had one reason for doing what he'd done. He had wanted to get rid of the tensions stirred by the business of the day. Purely a loosening-up process. He hadn't pretended anything else. It had nothing to do with her personally. She was just a handy female body to him—a desirable body that he had wanted to use.

With beautiful breasts.

Tessa smiled smugly to herself. She was sure that Blaize Callagan was very discriminating in his taste when it came to women. There was no need for him to have said that unless he meant it. She could rightly hug the compliment he had given her for the rest of her life. It made up for a lot.

She heard him sigh. He turned his head towards hers. "There is more to you than meets the eye, Stockton," he said.

"I'm an ordinary person, sir. With very simple needs," Tessa replied. Like a man to love her and stay faithful to her, as she would with him. But failing that, she at least had something exciting to remember.

In some perverse way—totally against all she had ever lived by—she was feeling an intensely primitive satisfaction in casting all her principles aside with Blaize Callagan. She wondered if there was an untamed beast in everyone underneath the skin of social strictures that ruled ordinary everyday life.

"Not at all, Stockton. I can't agree. You're complex," he said consideringly. "Very complex."

"If you say so, sir."

"Thank you for agreeing with me, Stockton." A touch of dry amusement there.

"My pleasure, sir," she answered sweetly.

His head turned away again and he lapsed into silence.

Tessa smiled. At least she had forced Blaize Callagan into a reassessment of her. She had surprised him. He hadn't expected her to be like that at all. She didn't imagine Blaize Callagan was presented with the unexpected very often. It had certainly got to him. He hadn't been able to switch his mind straight back to business. That was definitely a positive score for her. Not his way! Not *all* his way, anyhow.

However, no matter what had happened and how she felt, it behove her to keep things in perspective. When this conference was over, the parting of the ways would come. What she had just experienced with Blaize Callagan was memory material. No more than that. Something to tuck away in her mind and bring out with wonder occasionally. She mustn't get serious about it. The only serious thing to Blaize Callagan was business.

He heaved another sigh. "I don't know how you feel, Stockton, but I'm feeling very good. Very relaxed." His voice purred with satisfaction.

"Oh, limber, sir," she said airily. "I'm feeling very limber."

"Limber," he repeated appreciatively. "Your vocabulary is improving, Stockton."

"Thank you, sir."

"I think I'll go and look at that memo again."

Yes, it was back to business, all right. Tessa resigned herself to the inevitable, glad that she hadn't started fooling herself into hoping for any more from him. "Do you require any help from me, sir?"

"A cup of coffee would go fine."

"Black and two sugars, wasn't it, sir?"

"Good memory, Stockton."

"I try, sir."

He rolled over and kissed her. Very thoroughly. "I like the way you try, Stockton," he said.

Then he heaved himself off the bed, picked up his clothes and walked out of the bedroom. Which was not the bedroom designated for either of them. Tessa recollected her wits, which had been shattered by his kiss, and told herself to get moving, as well. If he could wander off naked, she supposed she could, so she picked up her clothes and made her exit from the bedroom. She didn't see him on her way to her own room.

The hotel provided bathrobes, which was handy because she hadn't packed her dressing-gown. She put on the terry garment and went to the kitchen to make the coffee. Having done that, she found Blaize seated at the computer. In his bathrobe. He certainly had fantastic legs.

"Thank you, Stockton," he said as she placed the mug on the table. He didn't look at her. He was concentrating on the monitor screen. Totally switched to business, she thought wryly, now that he was nicely relaxed.

"You can go to bed if you wish," he said. "It's been a very tiring day."

"Thank you, sir. It certainly has been tiring!" she said, with truly marvellous aplomb, particularly since she had a maniacal urge to hit him over the head with the nearest blunt object.

She took a deep steadying breath instead. She knew this was how it was. There was no point in wanting anything different from him. It wasn't going to happen. That was raw reality! But at least he wasn't pretending anything different, like Grant Durham! With Blaize Callagan, what you got was what you got. However, she did have the satisfaction of knowing that he would be more careful about underestimating her from now on. She was not just a handy female body.

Tessa picked up her glasses, her hairpins and rubber band, collected her suit jacket from the chair and went to her bedroom. She hung up her clothes, washed her face and went to bed. All of a sudden, she was very tired. She was asleep within seconds of her head hitting the pillow. Either she was totally exhausted or her mind was at peace. Her sleep was deep, uninterrupted and dreamless.

CHAPTER FOUR

"TIME TO RISE AND SHINE, Stockton!"

Tessa's eyelids flew open. Blaize Callagan stood in the bedroom doorway, resplendently handsome in a navy pin-striped suit, emanating the air of command that she had come to associate with him. For one fuzzy moment Tessa thought it had to be a dream. Then memory slashed across her mind, sparking a tide of heat that clothed her bare skin in a rosy flush.

His lips moved into that quirk, which she could now identify as amusement laced with knowingness. "It's seven-fifteen," he said. "Eight o'clock breakfast. I let you sleep as late as seemed viable."

Tessa found her tongue. "Thank you."

He looked at her for a few moments longer, gave that small decisive nod of his head, then moved off towards the living room.

Tessa wondered if she had passed his standard for how a woman should look the morning after. She shot out of bed, wrapped herself in the towelling robe and raced to the bathroom. The vanity mirror reflected a wild mane of rich brown hair, a face that was ironed free of fatigue and blooming with colour, and eyes that looked brighter and larger than usual. But since she didn't know what Blaize Callagan's standard was, she couldn't make any meaningful judgement.

Besides, it was irrelevant anyway. It wasn't as if he had any intention of making her a fixture in his life. Tessa told herself sternly that she mustn't lose sight of that. It was important to act accordingly. Pride and dignity and self-respect were all at stake here. Having never had an encounter before, Tessa wasn't too sure of the rules, but she suspected that one didn't refer to it unless the other party did.

Nevertheless, it was nice of him to let her sleep in, she thought, as she crammed her hair into a shower cap. It showed consideration. On the other hand, he probably hadn't needed her for anything. She mustn't fall into the trap of reading what she wanted to read into Blaize Callagan's actions or manner towards her. Any kind of emotional involvement was out.

She had had four years of emotional involvement with Grant Durham, and where had that got her? Betrayed, that's where! Betrayed and put down. She was going to keep her head around Blaize Callagan, no matter how lethally attractive she found him. She had only let him use her because she had wanted to use him. That was equality. She wasn't losing to him. She was finished with being a loser. From here on in, she was going to be a winner.

Tessa turned on the taps, tested the water temperature, then stepped under the stinging spray. A lot of very physical memories came flooding back as she soaped her body.

Two nights, Blaize had said.

Tessa had to admit to herself that she was now abandoned enough to want another experience with him. Totally shameless it might be, but a woman could be pardoned one encounter in a lifetime, couldn't she? So far she didn't have any regrets.

On the other hand, it was better not to take *two* nights for granted. He might have only said that to win his way last night. Be content with what you've had, Tessa admonished herself. Expect nothing. She who expecteth little is seldom disappointed. Much nicer to be surprised.

Satisfied that she had worked out the correct attitude to adopt for the day, Tessa turned off the taps, stepped out of the shower and set about producing a professional image.

Twenty minutes later she stepped into the living room, every hair wound into an immaculate topknot, makeup subtly perfect, glasses on, her three-hundred-dollar dark red business dress making the most of her figure with a simplicity of line that shrieked *class,* her black high heels freshly shined of every speck of dust.

"Ready, sir," she announced.

Blaize Callagan was standing in the doorway to the verandah, his back to her. He swung slowly around, a look of deep introspection lingering on his face before his eyes flicked into an acknowledgement of her presence.

"I trust you understand you are in a confidential position, Stockton," he said, the dark eyes boring into hers with commanding intensity.

Pride tightened her face and lifted her chin. Did he think she was going to blab to everyone that she had been to bed with him? Fiery indignation sparked a glittering resentment at him, but she disciplined her tongue to the terse little reply that gave him nothing to be critical about.

"Yes, sir," she said.

He nodded. "I've decided to play a lone hand today, Stockton. It's important that no one knows of the strategy suggested by that memo last night. The appearance of sincerity can best be maintained on our side by true belief. Therefore we let the cards fall where they will until only one play becomes possible. I've deleted the memo from the computer file. Delete it from your memory, Stockton."

"Yes, sir."

Tessa had to stifle a derisive laugh at herself. Business. Strictly business. If she had stopped to think about it, she should have realised that Blaize Callagan wouldn't give a damn about anyone knowing he had "relaxed" with her. It simply wasn't important to him.

"And what I said to you about sidestepping *ringi*..."

"Deleted, sir," Tessa assured him.

He relaxed. His eyes drifted down to her ankles and back up again, having gathered a warm gleam of appreciation. "Nice dress, Stockton."

"Thank you, sir."

His mouth slowly curved into a dazzling smile that curled Tessa's toes and did a lot of chaotic damage on the way to reaching her extremities.

"You've got style, Stockton," he said approvingly.

Tessa sternly repressed the heady rush of pleasure in his compliment. "It's nice of you to say so, sir," she said offhandedly.

One eyebrow lifted in sardonic inquiry. "You think I'm nice?"

"Oh, don't go overboard, sir. Your niceness is only a very small percentage of your total self. Trivial, really."

He stared incredulously at her for a moment, then burst into a peal of laughter. He looked so devastatingly handsome that all Tessa could do was stare at him and try desperately to keep her body and soul in one piece. He finally sobered, but his eyes kept dancing with some deep inner delight.

"Stockton, your vocabulary and ideas increase in leaps and bounds. A lot of hidden depth there. However, it's time to fortify ourselves with a substantial breakfast. This day will not only be exhausting, but quite draining."

"Yes, sir," Tessa agreed, feeling very pleased with herself. She had surprised Blaize Callagan again. She mentally chalked up another positive score. He would be even more careful in future about underestimating her.

Breakfast was a buffet affair, although a hot breakfast could be ordered. Blaize Callagan, of course, sat down and ordered. Milling along a line of people was not his style. Tessa, however, was attracted to the wide selection of fruits and croissants. Jerry Fraine joined her in the queue.

"How's it going, Tessa?" he asked.

"Fine, Jerry," she assured him. After all, she hadn't done anything that would reflect badly on him.

"What's on the agenda for today?"

The question slid out naturally, his expression completely bland and open. Which meant he was very keenly interested. Tessa knew Jerry Fraine too well not to recognise his probing tactics. However, in this instance her first loyalty was to Blaize Callagan, and he had sworn her to absolute discretion. On the other hand, she would be going back to being Jerry's secretary, so tact was definitely called for.

She smiled. "Jerry, if it's anything like yesterday, I think we're in for a lot of surprises."

His eyebrows shot up in amused inquiry. "Like what?"

She leaned towards him conspiratorially. "If you can get Mr. Callagan to tell you, then I'd appreciate it if you'd tell me. He keeps a lot to himself. I never know what's going to happen next."

It was the right touch. He gave a dry little laugh. "I know what you mean. Just hang in there, Tessa. And don't—"

"Stuff up," she finished for him.

Jerry grinned at her. "Are the glasses working?"

Tessa frowned. "I think he suspects something, Jerry."

He started chuckling and quickly coughed to cover up. "Just hang in there, Tessa. Don't let your guard down. Blaize Callagan is a great man, but . . . he could tear you apart."

It was friendly advice, she knew, and she appreciated his concern for her. "I can look after myself, Jerry," she assured him.

Jerry's eyes twinkled with some secret amusement. "I figured you could. Otherwise I wouldn't have . . ." He shrugged off whatever he had been going to say, then added, "He certainly didn't know what he was getting in you."

Tessa frowned at him. "Didn't you tell him?"

His face blanked out for a second, then projected wise experience. "Some things, Tessa, are better left for other people to find out for themselves," he said gravely.

That was true, she thought. It was no use telling anyone you could do things. It was better to show them you could. "Right," she agreed. "And thanks for recommending me, Jerry. I'm glad I got the chance to see how you people work."

They parted then and went to their separate tables. Blaize Callagan had a plate of eggs and bacon and sausages and tomato and mushrooms. He really meant "substantial," Tessa thought. She decided he would never bother saying what he didn't mean ... unless it had a business purpose.

Tessa did not enjoy the morning conference. It was certainly an education to watch the subtle shifts in top-level negotiations, but she could not help feeling disappointed in one specific outcome. Blaize Callagan seemed to be admitting total defeat. Although his men fought hard to put across their points, he sat with his shoulders slumped forward, projecting a listlessness that seemed totally out of character. Even when the Japanese delegation advanced some counter-proposal, he would wearily shake his head.

By mid-afternoon, the business conference had come to a premature conclusion. They were packing up, dejected, depressed, the usual courtesies hanging solemnly in the air like black thunderclouds.

Then Sokichi Nokumata, Blaize Callagan's chief opponent against *ringi*, made a suggestion about a project that was completely peripheral to the main deal. Tessa felt the instant tension flow in Blaize Callagan's body, saw the hard glitter come into his eyes. He gave the upward look of a man without any firm resolution, pondering the suggestion. Then suddenly negotiations were going full bore again.

The late afternoon session saw all Blaize Callagan's plans come to fruition. The Japanese delegates against *ringi* were all being siphoned off onto another project. Divide and conquer. This was a master deal maker at work. Tessa had never seen anything like it, not even from Jerry Fraine.

Only in hindsight did she begin to appreciate the tactics that had been outlined in the memo last night. And only now did she begin to appreciate the intricate and incisive mind that drove the man who had subtly engineered precisely what he wanted.

He had run into an immovable object, but he hadn't got hurt. Not Blaize Callagan. He had sidestepped it, waiting for all the cards to fall, until there was only one possible play left. The ultimate finesse was in bluffing his opposite number into laying down the losing card for Blaize Callagan to win.

Tessa had known he was the top gun, but now she knew why. She had known he was out of her league, and that knowledge was now confirmed beyond a shadow of a doubt. She might amuse him, surprise him on a very minor level and even stamp a pleasant memory into some tiny corner of his mind, but that was as far as it could ever go.

For a permanent relationship, Blaize Callagan would naturally choose a complementary top gun... like Candice. A secretary was just a secretary. But Tessa was glad she had had this encounter with him. A man like Blaize Callagan would certainly never come her way again. In a way, she felt privileged to have been given the opportunity to share a little drop of life with him.

And it wasn't over yet.

Maybe tonight...

Then again, maybe not.

He wasn't feeling tense any more. He had won.

He shared his victory with his colleagues, several of whom accompanied them to the cottage for further discussion on the new development. Tessa was not required to take notes. She fulfilled the role of hostess, seeing that drinks were refilled when required.

Dinner was a very relaxed affair, bonhomie flowing as freely as the wine. Blaize Callagan was riding a high. Tessa suspected that no woman—however close—could give him the charge he got from pulling off the kind of deal he had stage-managed today. It surprised her that he did not prolong their time at the dinner table beyond the serving of coffee. Nor did he invite anyone to the cottage with them. They set off alone.

He looked at the sky as though making an exhaustive study of it. "It's a fine night, Stockton," he remarked. "The stars shine more brightly here in this country than anywhere else in the world."

"Yes, sir. And congratulations on your success today, sir," she said with complete sincerity. "Your star is really in the ascendant at the present moment."

"Ah, there's many a slip 'twixt the cup and the lip, Stockton. It's not all tied up with pretty bows yet."

"You're well on your way, sir. And you do have some bows to tie."

"We got lucky, Stockton. That was all. We got lucky."

She slid him a mocking look. "Like being up half the night working on your strategy and ideas so you could get lucky?"

"It helps, Stockton. No more than that. Though as a general rule, I've found that the harder you work, the luckier you get."

Silence. It felt like a companionable silence. The dim lights from the grounds, the moon above... It would be very easy to dream hopeless dreams, Tessa thought. A hand brushing hers, taking it, holding it firmly. It kicked her pulse into overtime and gave her the courage to ask what curiosity prompted.

"What does it feel like..." She hesitated, searching for the right words.

"Well?" he prompted.

"When you bring off a coup like you did today, how do you feel?"

The pressure on her hand increased violently. He gave a derisive snort. His mouth curled with a savage irony she didn't understand. No answer was immediately forthcoming. He looked at the stars again, and his profile was sharply etched. Tessa had the impression of a man in angry defiance of the universe that beamed down on him. The silence went on. Tessa wished she hadn't asked. It had seemed a simple question, yet clearly he was having some difficulty in answering it.

When he did speak, his voice was low and husky. Tessa had to listen carefully to hear the words. "At first there is the elation and the triumph..."

"I can understand that," she encouraged.

"Which is quickly followed by a kind of flat feeling, hard to describe...perhaps emptiness."

That surprised Tessa. "Why?"

"I guess it's the journey that's important, not achieving the goal." His sigh held a weary disillusionment. "I've been to that particular well and drunk its waters so many times. Now it seems to be such a charade. What else is there left to do? Make deals bigger and bigger?"

He shrugged his shoulders. "People think it important that I do it, but sometimes I wonder. I wonder if there isn't something more, something that I've left behind."

Tessa pondered that. Had she been too hasty with Grant Durham? If the journey was more important than the goal, maybe she should consider forgiveness. Maybe what had happened was an expression of something gone wrong that needed to be put right. Perhaps it was all part of the learning curve between two people. They had come so far...

Then the image of that overblown floozy with her big melons billowed across Tessa's mind. No, that wasn't part of the learning curve, she decided savagely. No forgiveness. The end. *Finis!*

"What's wrong, Stockton?"

"Sir?"

"You're nearly twisting my fingers off."

"Sorry, sir."

She instantly relaxed her grip and would have pulled her hand away except that he held on. His fingers began stroking over hers in a soothing motion that didn't really soothe. It reminded her how sensual his fingers could be. However wicked and wanton it was, she couldn't help hoping that he would feel a need for her tonight.

"What's on your mind, Stockton?"

She couldn't tell him that. It was tantamount to asking. Definitely against the rules, Tessa decided. An encounter should just happen. One didn't ask for it.

"I was thinking about what you said." Which was certainly true.

"Well?"

"Well, what?" She had never really felt this kind of desire before. It was very distracting.

He slid her a sardonic look. "What's a man supposed to do with his life, Stockton? Give me the benefit of your wisdom and insight."

His voice was mocking and sarcastic. Tessa didn't like that. She might be a lightweight compared to Blaize Callagan, but her life was just as important to her as his was to him. "I doubt that you're ready for the answer yet, sir," she said loftily. "A few more years of preparation perhaps . . ."

"Don't be patronising, Stockton," he said irritably. "It doesn't become you."

It didn't become him, either, she thought with a jab of resentment. He might be godlike in a lot of respects, but that didn't mean other people shouldn't be given their share of worth and respect.

"Yes, sir," she said, not giving him any ammunition to criticise her.

"Look at the universe out there, Stockton. Open your mind to it. Doesn't it make you feel the need to achieve something?"

"No, sir." She didn't have any need whatsoever to prove anything to the universe. All she had ever wanted was a decent life with a man who loved her.

"Doesn't it make you feel small and insignificant and insubstantial?"

"No, sir."

"Why not, Stockton?" He sounded slightly puzzled, as though he couldn't comprehend such an attitude of mind.

"It takes something *really* big to make me feel small and insignificant and insubstantial." Like Grant Durham's floozy.

He gave a soft little laugh. "I like your style, Miss Stockton."

Tessa felt a ripple of deep satisfaction. He had granted her the respect of a title. Miss . . . She wondered if she would ever be a Mrs., and had a moment of black depression.

Only a moment, because they had reached the cottage and suddenly Blaize Callagan turned and lifted her onto the first step up to the verandah. Which put her face to face with him so to speak.

"I like your style very much," he purred as he took off her glasses, folded them and popped them into his breast pocket.

Then he kissed her. And the stars of the universe were completely blotted out as he explored the dark sweet cavern of her mouth. Tessa stopped thinking. Blaize Callagan's kiss didn't leave any space in her mind for thoughts. He filled it with a marauding host of sensations, and as he pressed her closer and closer to him, her body wantonly responded to the hard evidence of a need that Blaize had no intention of denying.

He had meant *two* nights.

CHAPTER FIVE

No SEDUCTIVE MOVES this time. No talking. No asking. Blaize swept Tessa off the verandah step and carried her straight to his bedroom, urgency in every stride, urgency in ridding both of them of clothes, pressing her naked body to the pulsating power of his, kissing her with hungry passion, hands working fast to free her hair from its constraint, burying his face in its luxuriant silkiness, arching her body into the hard muscularity of his, groaning a primitive satisfaction in the yielding softness of her femininity.

No holding back. No contest for control. He came with her as he lifted her onto the bed and took her as he kissed her, a swift urgent invasion, plunging for the hidden depths of her to fill them with him, to immerse himself in her.

It was a complete coupling. Whether it was a need in both of them to forget everything else, or whether their bodies were simply driven by age-old instincts, or whether there was some dark common chord of innate savagery that rose to meet and answer the demands they made on each other, Tessa neither knew nor cared.

There was an intense satisfaction in the way their bodies moved together, an exhilarating intimacy, a knowledge that went beyond reason, response and counter-response, a greed for every sensation possible, excitement exploding into more excitement, an ecstatic fulfilment in the climax that rushed upon both of them, a sense of bonding that was very real, however fleeting.

And it was fleeting.

Blaize separated himself from her. With gentleness. But decisively. He lay on his back, his body completely still except for the rise and fall of his chest as his breathing gradually slowed to a normal pace.

Tessa did not want to think tonight. She turned her head and watched him, wondering what thoughts were going through his mind. If he was thinking at all. Perhaps he simply let his mind go blank at such times as these.

Tessa knew she shouldn't resent his silence, or his absorption in himself. Yet it didn't feel right that they could be so close together one moment and so far apart the next. Perhaps it was against the rules of an encounter, but she wanted more from him. The kind of physical communion they had just shared screamed out for corresponding verbal communion.

"Does that help assuage the emptiness, sir?" she asked, careful to keep any emotional demand out of her voice.

"It helps, Stockton," he said quietly. "It helps a great deal."

He'd dropped the "miss" again. The message was crystal clear. She was back to being a body. One that had given him what he wanted, but only a body, nevertheless.

He turned his head and looked quizzically at her. "What about you?"

"Oh, I had a good time, thank you very much," she said airily. Although her heart felt like lead, for some reason.

He rolled onto his side and scrutinised her face, as though searching for something. There was a slight crease between his brows, suggesting that she presented a puzzle to him that he hadn't yet solved, and he didn't like anything eluding his ability to pigeonhole it. Even a slight gap in his all-knowing mind could not be tolerated.

Good, she thought fiercely. If for no other reason, you will remember me for that, Blaize Callagan, because I will not give you the satisfaction of pigeonholing me.

A gleam of purpose burned into the dark eyes. "I think what we need is a drink," he said.

"What a fine idea!" she said, but if he thought a drink would loosen her tongue, he could think again.

"Stay here, Stockton," he instructed. "I'll bring it in."

"Thank you, sir."

He heard the derisive note in the "sir" and shot her a sharp glance as he rose from the bed.

She gave him her best smile.

His eyes glittered appreciation of the ploy, but there was also a threat or a warning in the glitter. Blaize Callagan did not give up on what he went after. She had become a curiosity to him, and he wanted his curiosity satisfied.

He left the bedroom without bothering to don his bathrobe, totally unself-conscious about his nakedness. Tessa decided she wasn't going to be self-conscious about hers, either. It did seem rather stupid to even consider it after all that had gone on between them.

He returned a few minutes later with an opened bottle of yellow-gold wine and a couple of glasses.

Tessa sat up against the pillows. He smiled at her, obviously liking what he saw. Which was fine. Tessa liked what she saw of him, too. He poured the wine into the glasses and handed her one. Then he clinked her glass with his and smiled some more.

"A glass of wine and thou," he said.

"You forgot the loaf of bread," she answered dryly.

He laughed and stretched out on the bed beside her, looking supremely content with his world. "Tell me about yourself, Stockton," he invited, idly stroking her skin with his free hand.

"I'm twenty-four years old, and not one of the years that I've lived would interest you, sir," she said dismissively.

"Let me be the judge of that," he retorted with silky-smooth persuasion.

Tessa took a sip of the wine. It was silky-smooth, too, sweet, heavy with the taste of fruit, caressing her throat like liquid velvet. She suspected it was very heavy in alcohol content because even a taste of it sent an intoxicating buzz to her head.

"I don't like being a bore, sir," she said firmly, then took a smaller sip of the wine, testing its strength again. Liquid dynamite, she thought. But very, very nice. The slight chill on it made it all the more inviting, but she wasn't going to fall into that trap.

"How do you like the wine?" Blaize asked.

She looked him straight in the eyes and said, "Oh, I'm managing to choke it down, sir."

A flicker of outrage crossed his face, quickly followed by a dry, barely hidden contempt. "I will concede this isn't the most expensive wine in the world. The 1801 Margaux does cost more. So, too, does the

1795 Madeira." He twirled the wine around in his glass. "This is a mere '29 d'Yquem."

"Is that a fact, sir?" Tessa said with arch interest.

He took a sip, rolling the wine around in his mouth before swallowing it. "That's a fact," he said with heavy irony.

"And does such an expensive wine help to fill the emptiness, sir?" she asked curiously.

His expression underwent a lightning change, wiped clear of any trace of irony or contempt. His eyes bored into hers with a piercing brightness that would not be denied anything he wanted to know.

"You are a tease, Miss Stockton," he said softly.

"No, I am not, Mr. Callagan," she returned, her eyes defying his judgement. Then she smiled. "Although I will concede it's no hardship to choke down this wine. And I thank you for the privilege of tasting its unique quality. Such a luxury is not part of my ordinary life."

She took another sip, her eyes still challenging his over the rim of her glass. He watched her for so long, she took another sip because his intense scrutiny had somehow made her mouth go dry. Quite unconsciously, her tongue flicked out to lick her lips.

His gaze dropped to her mouth, simmered there for several moments, then he took another swallow from his glass and placed it on the bedside table. He leaned over and took her glass out of her hand and placed it on her bedside table. Sheer unholy wickedness danced in his eyes as he slid her down on the pillows. Then his mouth mingled with hers, savouring the taste of the wine on her tongue, playing a slow erotic dance that was more intoxicating than the wine.

He dipped his fingers into her glass and anointed her breasts with the sweet sticky liquid. It didn't stay there. And it didn't stop there. He used the d'Yquem all over her body, making trails for his mouth to follow, filling her navel like a miniature cup for him to drink from, making the rich wine a scented aphrodisiac, which drew him on to taste all of her, and Tessa was totally lost in a world of incredible eroticism, inescapably enthralled by what he was doing to her. He wove a silken web of sensuality that held her totally captive, all the more so because it was done with such delicacy, tenderness, exquisite pleasure.

She closed her eyes and floated on a gentle sea of undulating sensation, feeling her body flow with different currents of excitement, some high, some low, but all mesmerising in their intensity. She was boneless, utterly limp when he finally slid inside her, and he moved her body gently around his, stirring even sweeter rivulets of pleasure.

"Open your eyes," he commanded softly.

Tessa obeyed without thought, completely drawn into his will, his desire, his way. She had no idea what he saw in her eyes as he took his possession of her in slow deliberate strokes. He felt very deep inside her. He felt part of her. A necessary part. And she knew she would feel bereft when he left her.

She didn't want it to end. When it did, the pleasure of feeling his life essence mingling with hers was shot through with the pain of knowing that it didn't mean what it should. Another drop, that's all it was . . . and she closed her eyes as tears welled into them and overflowed.

"No, no," he murmured thickly, and gathered her up in his arms, holding her tightly to him as he rolled onto his side, cradling her against him, stroking her hair, trailing soft kisses around her temples. "Don't cry. Don't," he pleaded.

But she couldn't stop the tears from coming. Somehow the caring gentleness of his embrace made it harder, but she valiantly tried to stem the flow, knowing she was breaking the unspoken pact of an encounter.

"I'm... I'm tired. That's all," she choked out, desperately trying to explain away the ungovernable flood of desolate emotion.

He would never understand how wrong this was to her. That he should make her feel so possessed by him when he didn't want to possess her, except for a few moments that might fill his emptiness. Somehow it was a worse betrayal than Grant's, although she couldn't accuse Blaize of dishonesty. Or infidelity. But it hurt. And she wished he hadn't taken her like that. Wished he hadn't made her feel so much. It wasn't fair. Not when he meant nothing by it, apart from some brief gratification.

"Hush...it's all right," he murmured, turning onto his back, taking her with him so that she lay half-sprawled across his body.

He kept stroking her hair and her back in soft soothing caresses, and gradually Tessa was able to blink the tears back. The effort exhausted her, and she could not find the strength to move away from him. He didn't seem to mind.

I mustn't think about this, Tessa told herself. Better to blank out her mind. Just let it be. It was over. Already the past. He was only a warm body, in comfortable contact with hers. Her cheek was pressed over his heart. She listened to the deep heavy thud of it, let it fill the empty spaces she forced into her mind, and slowly there was nothing else left but the hypnotic thud of Blaize Callagan's heart and the rhythmic strokes of soft fingertips on her back.

A deep languor seeped through her body. Drowsiness clouded her dulled mind. She fell asleep without any awareness of it descending upon her. She had no knowledge of Blaize Callagan gently shifting her onto a pillow, tucking bedclothes around her, softly smoothing her hair away from her face. No knowledge of him watching over her as he finished the bottle of d'Yquem alone. No knowledge that he walked out to the verandah of the cottage, looked up at the stars—cold taunting pinpoints of light in the bottomless pit of black sky—and in a fit of deep frustration, hurled the empty bottle into the night.

She awoke to a soft caress on her cheek and found him sitting beside her in his bathrobe, smelling of cleanliness and his tangy-fresh after-shave lotion, his black hair slightly damp, his tanned skin shiny and stretched tautly over his beautiful facial bones, his dark eyes wary and watchful.

"It's time to get up," he said quietly. He nodded towards the bedside table. "I brought you coffee."

She was embarrassed to find herself still in his bedroom. Even more embarrassed by the memory of her weeping jag last night. "I'm sorry," she said, wrenching her eyes from his and struggling to rouse herself. "I didn't mean to...to..."

"It's okay. There's no great hurry. It's only just gone seven. I wanted time to talk to you before we go to breakfast."

Sheer panic coiled through Tessa's stomach. She wasn't ready to talk to him right now. She needed time to compose herself. "Yes, sir. When I'm dressed, sir, if you don't mind," she gabbled.

He frowned, impatience stabbing from his eyes. But he stood up, jammed his hands into the pockets of his bathrobe and paced away. "When you're ready then." He tossed the words at her from the doorway, left her to make an exit from his bed by herself. For which she was extremely grateful.

She noticed her bathrobe on the bed. He had brought it in for her as well as the cup of coffee. Both were marks of consideration that she hadn't expected from Blaize Callagan. But then he probably knew the rules of an encounter a lot better than she did. All the same, she appreciated both gestures very deeply.

Tessa scrambled out of bed, wrapped herself in the bathrobe and looked around for the clothes discarded last night. They weren't anywhere to be seen. Nor were her hairpins. She grabbed the cup of coffee and hurtled along to her own room. She found everything neatly laid on her bed. She shook her head in wondering disbelief. She would never understand Blaize Callagan. He was a man full of contradictions. The arrogant taker... and the considerate giver.

She gulped down the coffee and headed for the bathroom. It was just as well today was the last day, she thought. She was getting in too deep with Blaize Callagan. Far too deep. And it couldn't lead anywhere. It was even more paramount now that she keep her head or she would end up a very bad loser. It was bad enough that he would remember her crying. What she had to do now was make a graceful dignified exit from his life. If she was to keep her self-respect.

The bitterly ironic part of this encounter was that she had embraced it for the memories it would give her, yet as she stood under the shower and soaped off the lingering smell of d'Yquem from her skin, her mind sheered away from last night's experience. She knew it wasn't lovemaking, yet it had ended up feeling too much like lovemaking for her to take any comfort from the memory. It was too disturbing. Too close to the bone.

She hurried out of the shower and concentrated fiercely on getting herself under tight control. She brushed her hair hard, wishing she could brush the memory of his touch out of it. It had felt like a tender loving touch, but it couldn't have been. It was a relief to get it all twisted up into a topknot again.

The green dress, thank heaven, had a flared skirt. Blaize Callagan wouldn't have to lift her in and out of the helicopter. She couldn't have borne that casual intimacy after what she had shared with him. Her hand trembled so much it was difficult to apply her makeup with any real expertise, but she managed a fair job of it. She looked around for her glasses. Her heart sank when she remembered Blaize had put them in his coat pocket.

She couldn't go into his bedroom!

She stood frozen for several seconds, worrying how to deal with the problem. Then her distracted gaze caught them lying on her bedside table. Blaize had remembered them. Of course, she thought in savage recrimination. He remembered everything. He had a computer mind that she could never match. Never.

She snatched them up and put them on. Then she packed all her belongings and zipped up her suitcase. The end, she thought. Another chapter in her life finished. Two chapters in one week. It had been a very eventful week. But at least this chapter could be finished with some style. Blaize liked her style. She would not let herself down—or him—by going out on anything less than a stylish note.

She found him in the same place he had been the previous morning, standing in the doorway to the verandah, looking out over a valley lit by bright morning sunshine. He wore a light grey suit today, impeccably tailored to fit his powerful physique.

Tessa paused for a few moments, remembering how she had run her fingers through the thick black hair, how her arms had clung around the strong column of his neck, how he had shuddered when she had run her fingernails over his back, how she had clutched his taut buttocks when...

She shut her eyes and willed the memories away. It was over, she reminded herself. Over. She swallowed hard, composed herself into businesslike practicality and forced herself to speak.

"I'm ready, sir."

He swung around, his face alight with a warmth she had never seen before. The dark eyes gleamed with pleasure as they ran over her dress. "Green suits you," he said softly.

His voice felt like a caress on her skin. "Thank you, sir," she said stiltedly.

He smiled, amusement twinkling in his eyes. "I need some more help from you, Miss Stockton."

"Yes, sir?"

"I seem to have developed a bad case of emptiness. I don't think two nights are enough."

There was a rush of blood to her head as she realised he didn't want to be finished with her. Then it drained slowly away as the reality of what he was asking hit home. More of the same. And she couldn't take it. It was a losing play all the way.

"I'm sorry, sir, but enough is enough. You've had your emptiness quota from me, sir," she said firmly, determined not to let her voice shake. It was bad enough that she felt so weakly tremulous inside.

He gave her an appealing smile. "Stockton, you can't walk out on me like this."

The dropping of the "miss" hardened her resolve. Her tawny gold eyes glittered into metallic defiance. "Oh, yes, sir, I can. That's precisely what I'm doing."

His eyes narrowed. He shook his head. "I don't believe you mean that."

"In a very short space of time, you'll come to believe it, sir," she said.

He stared at her for several seconds, the dark eyes projecting the dominance of his will. Then very deliberately he dropped his gaze, running it slowly down her body, burning through the green dress to remind her of every intimacy she had allowed him to take.

Tessa could do nothing to prevent the melting heat that radiated through her in debilitating waves. He could take her again now, and she wouldn't want to stop him. But she could and would control her future. There was no place in her future for a man who only wanted to use her, particularly when that man could hurt her as Blaize Callagan could. Not that he knew it. And she didn't intend that he should know it. She simply knew that he would never give her the kind of loving permanent relationship she wanted with a man.

His eyes returned to hers in blazing challenge. "Miss Stockton, are you seriously suggesting I'm not good enough as a lover for you?" he asked silkily.

Tessa took a deep breath. "Please don't feel put down, sir." She managed a dry little smile. "If I were writing a book on the rich and famous, and giving point scores for lovers, you'd score very highly."

"So?" he shot at her, as though she had just proven his point.

Tessa shrugged. "These things are interludes in life. It's run its course, sir. Better to accept that and get on with our real lives. I'm sure, if you stop to think about it, sir, you'll agree with me."

"And what if I don't?" he asked softly.

"Perhaps you should give it some more thought, sir. It would be best for both of us if you do agree." She pushed her lips into an appealing smile. "I'd prefer to remember it ending well."

He retracted the challenge from his eyes. It was replaced by a wry appreciation. He slowly returned her smile. "I do like your style, Stockton."

"Thank you, sir."

He walked over to her, rested his hands lightly on her shoulders and pressed a warm kiss on her forehead. "And thank you . . . for the interlude," he said softly.

"My pleasure, sir," Tessa managed huskily, desperately willing tears back from her eyes.

"So let's go tie up the Japanese," he said, a purposeful briskness in his voice.

Back to business, Tessa thought.

It helped.

No doubt about it. She had made the right decision. But she didn't feel like a winner.

Tessa didn't know how she managed to walk to the hotel for breakfast. Her legs performed miracles. She ate some breakfast, but if anyone had asked her afterwards what she had had, she wouldn't have been able to recollect any part of it. Fortunately the demands of the morning session with the Japanese forced her to concentrate on her shorthand. She was a good secretary and proud of it. And life would be back to normal tomorrow.

Lunch was devoted to wind-up pleasantries. Two deals had been tied up. Everyone was happy. The glow of a successful conclusion to the conference was on every face. Except Tessa's. However, she did manage to look cool, calm and collected.

At two o'clock the helicopters started arriving. A hotel porter took down a trolley of luggage. The pilots stowed it all away. Farewells were taken. The company men took off in their helicopters first. Blaize Callagan was the last to take leave of the Japanese delegation. He automatically took Tessa's arm to walk her down the slope of lawn. As soon as they were on the flat she disengaged herself and boarded the helicopter without Blaize's help. He took his seat by the pilot and they lifted off.

They might have been strangers, Tessa thought, for all the attention he had paid to her since leaving the cottage before breakfast. He had treated her with distant courtesy, no more, no less.

It was the same when they landed in Sydney. He helped her into the waiting limousine, sat beside her and studied documents from his attaché case. It reminded Tessa that she hadn't transcribed any of her notes from yesterday, and there were all those from this morning, as well.

She cleared her throat. "Mr. Callagan..."

"Mmm...yes, Stockton?" He belatedly lifted his head, as though dragged against his inclination to look inquiringly at her.

Tessa flushed in painful self-consciousness. "All the notes ... shall I type them up when I get back to the office?"

"They're in Rosemary's attaché case, aren't they?"

"Yes, sir."

"They'll be put safely aside in case they're needed. Whoever's been appointed my temporary secretary can transcribe from the tapes. No need for you to do any more, Stockton, unless we run into some audio problem. In which case, my secretary will call on you," he said dismissively, and returned his attention to his documents.

Tessa turned her face to the window, trying her utmost to ignore him as thoroughly as he could ignore her. This was what she had insisted upon. Complete cutoff. She could have had him as a lover...

No regrets, she told herself savagely.

That was the main rule of an encounter.

She had made the right decision. The way Blaize had cut it all dead from this morning was convincing enough proof of that. So no regrets.

The car pulled up outside the CMA building in North Sydney. Blaize packed away his documents and looked inquiringly at Tessa again.

"Where do you live, Stockton?"

Heat raced into her cheeks again. Did this mean ...

"No point in you coming in to the office for these last couple of hours. I'll take Rosemary's case with me. As it is, you've worked overtime the last few days. I'll give the driver your address so he can take you home," he said pleasantly.

Fool! she berated herself. She bit out where she lived and watched him leave the car, aching for something more from him, even though she knew it couldn't be expected. He spoke to the driver, held up his hand in a last brief salute to her, then strode into the building without a backward glance.

Finis.

The car moved off, taking her to the apartment she had left on Sunday night, the apartment she had shared with Grant Durham. She dragged her mind back to her real life.

The interlude was over.

She had a wedding to call off.

CHAPTER SIX

TESSA'S APARTMENT was in Neutral Bay, very handy to her work place in North Sydney. It was only a ten-minute drive from the office, although the trip took longer by the bus route. The bad news was fairly evident as soon as she walked in to the living room. While Grant was not physically present, his belongings still remained. He hadn't heeded her ultimatum.

Tessa felt sick at the thought of having to face him. Worse still, it was obvious from the state of the apartment that Grant meant to try for a reconciliation. It was clean and tidy. For Grant Durham, unbelievably so, after three days' occupation by himself.

Grant hated housework. He tidied up and did a few household chores only when Tessa took a firm stance about it. Nothing was ever done without her asking. He never picked up her clothes or brought her morning coffee like... But there was no point in thinking about Blaize Callagan. The niceties of an encounter were one thing, the niceties of a relationship quite another. All the same, Blaize had been good to her in that respect.

The fact that Grant had gone to so much trouble, even to a vase of fresh flowers on the table, was a sure sign that he was angling for forgiveness. She noticed, with grim distaste, that the bed was made up with fresh sheets and pillow slips. It was a bit late for common decency, Tessa thought savagely. She wasn't sure she could ever sleep in that bed again without remembering that woman. She was absolutely certain she could never share any bed with Grant again.

There was only one thing to do, she decided. Pack all his things for him before he got back from work. She would present him with a fait accompli, which would leave him as little ground as possible to stand on. As far as she was concerned, he had no ground at all, and she would tell him that in a few well-chosen words.

The packing served to keep her mind off Blaize Callagan, but it evoked a lot of other memories that she could have well done without; clothes that she had lovingly bought for Grant, mementoes of good times they had shared together, books and music tapes they had both liked. Several times she paused and wondered if she was doing the right thing.

Then she remembered how Grant had kept her dangling at his convenience, blowing hot and cold over the years, not even buying her an engagement ring when he had finally come to the point of suggesting marriage. The good times had been good, but she had tolerated a lot of bad for the sake of the good.

There had been other women in the past, but Grant had sworn all that was behind him. For him to have had that woman in her bed seven weeks before the wedding! Tessa wondered what she would have done if she had found that happening seven weeks *after* she was married. She shuddered at the thought.

Besides, after her encounter with Blaize Callagan, to be absolutely honest with herself, Grant just didn't measure up. At least not in that particular way. Tessa wondered if anyone ever would. It was a singularly bleak thought.

Tessa was sitting at the table in the living room when Grant walked in. He saw the suitcases and boxes piled up in the small lobby first, so he was prepared for her decision before actually facing her. The strange part was, Tessa felt nothing when she saw him, no anger, no revulsion, no outrage, no regret, no love, not even a remnant of liking. He was almost a curiosity.

There he was, a well-made man of above average height, well-dressed in a fawn business suit, a successful insurance salesman, intelligent and street-smart, very presentable in any situation. His sun-streaked blond hair had a natural wave that lent his rough-handsome face a lot of charm. Not that he needed extra charm. Charm oozed from Grant Durham. As it did now. His hands lifted in a gesture of apologetic appeal, his green eyes begging Tessa to believe she was the only woman who was special to him.

She felt nothing.

Four years of single-minded devotion to this man wiped out by a brief encounter with Blaize Callagan. Her mind said it was wrong that it should have happened...but it was no use denying that it had. She looked at Grant and it was as if a curtain had been rung down between them. The show was over and there was only emptiness.

"What can I say?" he began.

"Nothing," she replied flatly.

He walked over to her, sat down at the table, struck a confidential pose. "Tessa, we can talk this through—"

"No, we can't, Grant," she cut in. "We're finished. Quite finally this time."

"Tessa, that woman...she meant nothing to me—"

"Then why take her to bed?"

"It was a strange encounter. Nothing to it. It just happened."

"In *my* bed? It just happened in *my* bed?"

He saw the battle light in her eyes and hastily retreated. "Let me rub your shoulders and back. You've been under a lot of tension."

"NO!" Tessa said it in capital letters.

"There's an explanation for this . . ."

"I don't want to hear it. I simply don't care any more. Nothing you say will make any difference to me. You'll be wasting your breath."

He shook his head in pained protest. "I can't believe you would change like this."

"It's because I believe you *won't* change that I'm like this," she replied stonily.

"Unbelievable."

"Believe it!" she said harshly.

Why did men have trouble believing anything they didn't want to hear from a woman? Blaize had been the same this morning. Didn't they think a woman could know her own mind?

Grant composed his face into an appeal for reason. "Look, I've gone and had some therapy over this."

"You've what?" Tessa looked at him in astonishment. Was he serious? Doubts sliced into her mind again. Perhaps she was being too hasty in condemning him. Four years of her life . . . and encounters did happen, as she had just experienced herself. But not if you were happy with someone else. Or committed to someone else, as Grant had supposedly been committed to her.

"I wanted to make amends," he said. "So I've had therapy."

The words slid out a bit too glibly to Tessa's mind. She looked at Grant suspiciously. "What did the therapist say?"

"Well, she said that what we've got to do is start touching again—"

Instant recoil. "NO!"

"—physically, so that our minds can meet," he added persuasively.

Revulsion at the very thought. "NO!"

"And that will help you get over your bitter black jealousy."

Tessa stared incredulously at him. Suspicion gradually hardened into bleak cynicism. "Your therapist," she said sarcastically, "told you that it's all my fault?"

"Well, in a way it is," he said, looking at her with soft sympathetic eyes. "I mean, I'm not jealous of you, Tessa. You're the one who's jealous of me."

No contrition. Not even a guilty conscience, let alone repentance.

"My black jealousy," she said softly, the anger beginning to seethe again.

Grant nodded. "Your black jealousy. It's a character defect in many people—"

"I'm not jealous!" It was the breaking point.

"Yes, you are."

"That's the last straw, Grant!" she yelled at him, leaping up from the table and storming around the room in fulminating rage, her hands gesticulating her furious rejection of him. "What we had is broken and can't be fixed. Ever again. I'll cancel all the wedding arrangements. There's nothing you need do except go. You're free again, to do whatever you want, to whomever you want, wherever you want."

"I want you, Tessa. You know I've always come back to you. I always will come back to you. You're the one..."

He rose from his chair and tried to catch her arms. Tessa beat him away.

"No! No more! Leave me alone. Find someone else to come back to. I don't want to talk about it. Go screw some other floozy. But not in *my* bed! Not ever again!"

"Tessa...come on, now...change your mind."

The indulgence in his voice only inflamed her rage. "I'm not going to!"

"Why not?"

She flung it at him recklessly. "Because I've started an affair with someone else!"

His face went white. "You slut!" And he hit her a ringing blow across the side of her face.

She stood still, her chest heaving, her eyes dilating as she fought for control. "Black jealousy, Grant," she taunted him bitterly. "You'd better get some more therapy."

He ranted. He raved. He tried tears. Crocodile tears, since they were soon blinked back when they didn't win any softening from her. Tessa stared at him stony-faced, giving him no encouragement whatsoever, projecting total indifference. It wasn't hard. It was precisely what she felt. Eventually Grant realised he was faced with a brick wall and he hadn't made the slightest crack in it.

"You're a bitch, Tessa," he said resentfully.

"I wonder why?" she mocked. "You'll find no more joy here, Grant. This is what's called irretrievable breakdown. Quit while the going's easy. The longer you stay, the harder I'll get. I'll even call the police to get you out of my life.''

"No need for that," he snarled at her.

He went.

It wasn't a gracious exit.

Tessa didn't care. He was gone. That was all that mattered. There was still the unpleasant task of calling off the wedding, but apart from weathering her mother's recriminations, that was just mechanics. The truth of the matter was, she had had a lucky escape from being tied to a man who wasn't worth being tied to. She was glad Grant was gone, glad that she wasn't going to be his wife. But she wasn't glad to be free. She wanted to be loved. Truly loved.

Tessa did sleep in her bed that night. It didn't seem to matter any more. Somehow seeing Grant again—feeling nothing for him—made last Sunday's infidelity completely meaningless. It had simply been the straw that had broken the camel's back, her back. The burden that Grant Durham had placed upon her had become too great to carry.

She lay in the darkness wondering if that meant she had fickle emotions. For the first time she felt unsure and insecure about the future. Not with the decision she had made about Grant Durham. That was inevitable, given the way she felt. The path into the future, though, was very dark, very obscure and very unnerving. Or was that what encounters did to people—rearranging their perspectives and making everything look different and feel different?

It was not the same for men, Tessa decided. They seemed able to go from woman to woman without getting at all emotionally affected by it. Just sex. Blaize Callagan had obviously liked the sex he'd had with her and wanted more of it. To say he wanted to be her lover... that was a misnomer if ever she'd heard one. He wasn't offering love. He simply found her body's response to his very satisfying. Enough to prolong the experience for a while.

Tessa stifled her stupid desire for more of him with the thought that he would soon find someone else to satisfy him. He probably had someone else all the time. A lot of someone elses. A man like Blaize would never have to look far for that kind of satisfaction.

He hadn't cared about her as a person. She was just the nonentity called Stockton. The person whose vocabulary was limited to "yes, sir," so that she wouldn't get into trouble. Stockton. Hardly a person. Just a thing. The darkness of the future loomed even larger.

Tears welled into her eyes and she turned her face into the pillow and cried. It didn't matter if she shed tears tonight. There was no one to see her. No one to hear her. No one to comfort her. She was alone, and felt more alone than she had in her whole life.

The lesson was clear, she told herself. Encounters were not her style. She had been mad to think she could handle such an interlude. If it hadn't been for Grant's infidelity...

No. She couldn't justify her behaviour on that alone. Although if Grant hadn't done what he had, she would never have responded to Blaize Callagan, no matter how attractive she found him. One thing led to another with the strangest results.

In the end she didn't regret what had happened. Blaize Callagan had got to her. In a way that no other man had. She didn't regret having known him. She regretted that she was not the right kind of woman to suit him. Like Candice. Full of flair, sophistication and bright red waves of tossing, tempestuous hair.

The next morning Tessa made no attempt to create a professional image. She was herself again. Back to square one, back to go, back to her real life, and the sooner she started getting on with it the better, she told herself sternly.

The first thing would be an exotic holiday somewhere as soon as she had cancelled the wedding. Time to form new memories. Time to heal. Time to forget. Perhaps a cruise around the Pacific islands. Or anything else. It didn't matter what she chose. She had four weeks' leave coming up—for the honeymoon she wouldn't have—and she certainly wasn't going to spend it moping around alone at home, thinking of what might have been, or what should have been happening.

Tessa mentally squared her shoulders and prepared to face the new day. As she entered the CMA building she refused to think Blaize Callagan was also on the premises. He had nothing to do with her real life.

Jerry Fraine looked surprised to see her at her desk when he arrived at the office. He raised his eyebrows in quizzical fashion. "I thought I'd have to manage without you until Rosemary Davies returned," he remarked.

Tessa returned her own surprise. "You did say I was only needed for the conference, Jerry."

He gave a quirky little smile that seemed to express some inner satisfaction. "Well, I'm glad you're back with me. I don't suppose the conference went quite the way Blaize Callagan expected," he added musingly, "but in the end we managed."

"I think he was pleased with the result," Tessa said.

"So he should be. We got lucky this time. Real lucky. Not even Blaize Callagan could have anticipated this result."

He went into his office, and Tessa thought that if she told Jerry Fraine what had really happened, he would get the shock of his life. But Blaize Callagan wanted that kept confidential and that was the way it was going to be.

She idly wondered if Blaize might have been briefly piqued by her rejection of him as a lover. Decided against it. He had succeeded in getting what he wanted from the Japanese delegation. That was the important thing to him.

Although he had seemed to have some doubts about its importance on the second night. But by that time, Tessa thought cynically, he'd already achieved what he had set out to achieve. What was the phrase for it? Post coitus tristesse? After sex the sadness. She figured that all great men probably had the occasional doubts about what they were doing, but it didn't stop their will to achieve.

Jerry poked his head around the door between their offices. "I wonder..." He gave a funny little laugh. "I wonder about a lot of things. As you so aptly remarked, Blaize Callagan keeps a lot to himself. Very difficult to know what he's thinking. Or what he's doing. Or what he's done."

"Yes," Tessa agreed.

"Any comment?"

"No."

"That's what I thought." He seemed to be pleased with himself. "So he did get up to tricks."

"Jerry, you mustn't make inferences like that."

He immediately changed the subject. "Is the wedding on again?" he asked curiously.

"No." She gave him a mocking smile. "It was a full-scale rift, Jerry. Not a tiff. We said our final goodbyes last night."

"Oh!" His face softened into sympathy. "Sorry about that. I guess this has been a bad time for you."

"I'll survive," she said airily. "There's a lot more fish in the sea. That's what people always say to you at a time like this. I've decided to go on a Pacific cruise and look them over. See if there's one waiting with its mouth open to be caught."

He relaxed into an approving grin. "Good for you, Tessa!"

Jerry was in excellent humour all day. He had figured out what really happened at the conference, and he made Tessa feel valued and appreciated with extra little courtesies. It helped.

That night she rang her sister. Sue was seven years older than Tessa, happily married with a husband who adored her and two beautiful children. Because of the age difference, Tessa had been deprived of any real sisterly companionship while growing up, but in recent years she'd forged a closer understanding with Sue.

That was why she had gone to her place on Sunday night to take refuge from Grant's occupation of her apartment. At this stage, Sue represented a more sympathetic person to talk to than her mother would be. There was not so much of the generation gap that seemed totally unbridgeable with her mother.

"I'm calling the wedding off," she told her sister bluntly.

"Thank God you've come to your senses at last!" came the approving reply. "You should have called it off with Grant years ago."

"You didn't like him?" Tessa asked weakly. She hadn't known.

"He never appreciated you, Tessa. For heaven's sake, having made the decision, don't backslide now. Don't let him talk or pressure you into going back to him."

"You never said anything like this before."

"You wouldn't have listened. No point in saying anything. People never take advice about their love life. I can say it now because it's not advice. I'm glad you've woken up in time. Never thought you would. Grant Durham wasn't husband material, Tessa."

"No. I guess he wasn't. It still hurts a bit though."

"Better to hurt now than to cost you later."

"I suppose so. Will you back me up when I tell Mum? I'm not looking forward to that."

"Mum wears rose-tinted spectacles. She is incapable of seeing harm in any handsome man. Lack of judgement. If she calls me, I'm all on your side."

"Thanks, Sue."

"Pleasure. And if you're feeling miserable, pop over. You're welcome any time."

"Mum's going to be upset about this. There's no way of avoiding it."

"Mum wasn't going to marry the jerk. You were."

Tessa recoiled from that description of Grant. It was wounding to her pride, if nothing else. "I didn't know that you thought Grant was a jerk."

"He was."

Tessa sighed. "Oh, well, with my luck with Mum..."

"If she throws a tantrum, remember one thing."

"What?"

"You would have copped the consequences. She wouldn't."

"Thanks, Sue."

"My pleasure."

They ended the call on this note of mutual understanding.

For the rest of the evening Tessa managed to keep Blaize Callagan out of her mind by reviewing her relationship with her mother. Which wasn't good. Her mother criticised everything she did, and always had. Nothing was ever right or proper. Her mother was sixty years old—Tessa had been a late child—and the world had changed a lot since she was young. Tessa's father had kept up with it, more or less, but her mother... there just didn't seem to be a meeting place between them.

Tessa tried. She loved her mother. It wasn't that she deliberately courted her disapproval. Basically she wanted what her mother had. A good marriage. The manner in which this purpose could be accomplished had altered so dramatically in the last forty years that the rules applicable then were no longer applicable now.

Her mother didn't seem to understand. Women did have to work, did have to have a job to help pay off the mortgage. Men couldn't survive financially without their women to help. And men had to respond by looking after their women differently. Her mother didn't understand that, or a lot of other things, either, like sex. Disapproval of Tessa's live-in relationship with Grant had soured many things between her mother and herself. At least, now, that was at an end.

Tessa wished it was as simple as it seemed to have been in her mother's day, but the clock couldn't be turned back. Fashions were different, hairstyles were different, music was different, the kind of social life people enjoyed now was different...all different. Women earned good enough wages to afford choices that hadn't been available forty years ago. Tessa didn't need a man to support her, not financially. But she wanted one to stand by her side and share her life, just as her mother had. That was one common ground between them.

The next morning Tessa packed her bag for the weekend. She would catch the commuter train to Gosford after work. Her parents were expecting her because it had been arranged that the invitations to the wedding were to be written out. They were expecting Grant to come with her, as well, and in that respect, they were in for a major surprise. They certainly wouldn't be expecting the announcement she had to make, but she resolved to be very patient with her mother and try to reach a better understanding.

The day passed quite pleasantly at the office. Tessa liked being busy and Jerry had a lot of work for her to do. She was with him in his office, taking notes for a memo, when a call came through from Blaize Callagan's office, demanding Tessa's presence forthwith. It was four o'clock, only one hour left in the working week.

Jerry looked at her speculatively.

"They must want me to translate some of my shorthand notes," she said, doing her best to ignore the ebb and flow of colour in her cheeks.

It couldn't possibly mean anything else, she argued fiercely to herself. It was utterly absurd for her heart to be pounding like a jackhammer. She would only be seeing his secretary, not *him*. Even if she did see *him,* he would only treat her in the same offhand manner as he had before. Their intimate interlude would not be referred to in any way, shape or form.

Jerry gave her a dry little smile. "Got your glasses, Tessa?"

She groaned as she realised her present appearance fell far short of the professional image she had created for Blaize Callagan. "I left them at home, Jerry."

Not only that, she was wearing a black miniskirt and a red T-shirt, which was bunched around her waist, pulled in by a dark burgundy leather belt. Having been in a hurry because of having to pack a bag this morning, she had simply slid side combs into her hair above her ears, and her only makeup was a dash of lipstick, which was probably eaten off by now.

"What am I going to do?" she cried in dismay.

Jerry chuckled. "Oh, I daresay you can carry it off, Tessa. No doubt you've already given Blaize Callagan a surprise or two. He's got a strong heart. He'll survive one more."

"You don't mind him seeing me like this?"

"Why should I?"

"Because I'm your secretary. I thought you didn't want me to let you down."

He laughed outright. "Not over how you look, Tessa. No man in his right mind could possibly object to how you look. Don't worry about it. Just go. Blaize Callagan doesn't like to be kept waiting."

She went.

Anyone who worked for CMA did not say no to a summons from Blaize Callagan. Tessa had no choice but to go. But there were some things that she could say no to. And she would. If she had to.

Not that it could be about that, Tessa told herself. It was silly to even think about it. In fact, she mustn't think about it. Not if she was to carry off this unexpected meeting with any style.

CHAPTER SEVEN

ON THE WAY UP in the elevator she rearranged her T-shirt around her belt, making sure it was at least evenly pouched. It wasn't a raggy T-shirt, she consoled herself. It was top quality. She wished her skirt wasn't quite so short, but there wasn't anything she could do about that. Besides, she did have good legs. Which was why she favoured miniskirts. Although this one wasn't as short as some. Only a few inches above the knee. It wasn't as if it was indecent.

She licked her lips, hoping that if there was any lipstick left, a bit of moisture might help heighten the colour. She didn't think Blaize had been fooled about the glasses, anyway. Besides which, Jerry didn't mind about her appearance, and she had told Blaize she was going back to her real life. This was her real-life image. He could take it or leave it.

Undoubtedly he would leave it.

She was crazy even to be thinking like this. Blaize Callagan had already put aside his interest in her. She didn't want what he had offered her anyway.

She wished her heart would stop beating so fast. Her skin was beginning to feel clammy. She wiped her hands on her skirt as the elevator doors opened onto his floor. Cool, calm and collected, she told herself, then tilted her head high, squared her shoulders and stepped out.

Two women were in the outer reception area, obviously packed up and ready to go home, their handbags slung over their shoulders. One was the receptionist Tessa had met briefly on Monday morning. The other was probably the temporary secretary replacing Rosemary Davies. They both looked at Tessa with sharp curiosity.

"I'm Tessa Stockton," she forced out. "Mr. Callagan..."

"Go straight in," the receptionist invited. "Mr. Callagan is waiting for you, Miss Stockton."

Tessa was well aware of their eyes boring after her as she went in to the managing director's office. It was clear now that she hadn't been asked up here to transcribe her notes. Which meant... what?

Blaize Callagan was standing at the picture window, which gave him a view over Sydney Harbour. The afternoon sunshine struck his face in a way that highlighted the spare purity of his bone structure, like a perfect Greek sculpture. His eyes, however, were not the lifeless eyes of marble or wood or stone. The moment Tessa shut the door behind her they were burning over her, devouring her with such vibrant intensity that her insides turned instantly to jelly.

Her clothes were totally irrelevant. She knew he wasn't seeing her clothes. He was stripping her naked. Remembering. Heat scorched over her skin in prickling waves. Pride insisted that she stop him from reducing her to a body like this. She swallowed hard then forced her tongue to work.

"You wanted me, sir?"

It was a most unfortunate choice of words. As soon as they were out Tessa would have given anything to retract them. They hung in the air between them, gathering sizzling overtones and undertones while Tessa squirmed in agonised mortification. To give him such a lead-in was tantamount to an invitation, and that wasn't what she had meant at all.

"Yes," he said, his lips moving into that sensual quirk that knew too much. "Yes, I do want you," he added slowly.

He would have her here, right here in this office, if she let him. His suit coat was off. His tie was loosened. The top two buttons of his shirt were undone. His stance was all aggressive male, confident of his power to attract her, to stir the same desire he felt, to command her response.

His strong sexuality was reaching her in waves, determined on drawing her to him. That was why he had dismissed his closest ancillary staff. He wanted to be alone with her, without fear of interruption. Any second now he would say he needed her. Needed her very much.

He lifted a hand.

Tessa stiffened. The door was just behind her. She didn't have to stay—wouldn't stay—if he started approaching her. She was not going to be used like that, not by anybody.

He waved an invitation towards the chair in front of his desk. "I want to talk to you," he said quietly. Soothingly. As though he could read what she was thinking and was subtly backing off.

Tessa hesitated. She didn't like the idea of sitting down while he was standing up. The last time they were in that situation he had taken advantage of it. No, it was better if she remained on her feet and near the door. Besides which, she wasn't sure her legs would carry her over to the chair with the dignity she was determined on maintaining.

Her eyes challenged his. "What would you like to talk about, sir?"

He sighed and turned away from her, walking to the front of his huge executive desk. He swung slowly around to face her again, then propped himself against the desk and folded his arms, deliberately adopting a relaxed and nonthreatening pose.

"We have a problem, Stockton," he said. "If you'd be so obliging as to sit down, I'd like to discuss it with you."

She remembered how he had used body language to great effect with the Japanese delegation. Blaize Callagan was a master of it. What was in his mind was not necessarily what he portrayed at all. Yet she was also aware of his ability to switch on and off. Perhaps he had stopped remembering and actually did have some business to discuss with her. In an ultimate sense, he was her boss.

Tessa sent a shot of willpower to her shaky legs and moved to the chair. She sat down, extremely conscious of her short skirt and the amount of thigh she was showing. However, Blaize Callagan kept his gaze fixed on hers. Which reassured her. Slightly.

"Yes, sir?" she said, inviting him to state the problem.

The dark eyes bored into hers, commanding her full attention. "It's not working, Stockton," he stated softly.

"What's not working, sir?"

"Parting the way we did. I have given it more thought, and I can't agree."

Tessa's heart leapt. "Can't agree with what, sir?"

"We haven't run our course, Stockton. As far as I'm concerned, we've barely started running our course. I want you to spend the weekend with me. I have a boat moored at Akuna Bay. I'll take you cruising around the Hawkesbury River. Just the two of us together. For the whole weekend. Agreed?"

Tessa was torn by temptation. A whole weekend with Blaize Callagan. No business. Just the two of them getting to know each other. Except he only wanted to know her in the biblical sense. A weekend of saturation sex. That's what it would be. Another interlude. And this was one weekend when she had to face real life.

"I'm sorry, sir. I have other plans for this weekend," she said, her tawny gold eyes mocking his disinterest in her real life. He hadn't asked if she was available. He arrogantly assumed that his time was more important than hers and she would fall in with his plans.

"Cancel them, Stockton."

The command in his eyes riled resentment. "Oh, I am cancelling them, sir. All the plans I've made for years. I realise you don't know about them. I realise you don't care about them. But other people do. Particularly my parents."

She smiled sweetly. "You see, sir, I'm going home to cancel my wedding. I can't leave it any later. Six weeks is the cut-off point. The obligatory notice one has to give or pay the penalty of financial loss on the arrangements. I don't want to put that on my parents, as well as the costs they've already incurred on my behalf. So, quite simply, I'm not free this weekend."

Shock tightened his face. His eyes sharpened, drilling into hers with urgent intensity. "This wedding,

Stockton. Is it being put off because of me?'' he asked quietly.

Tessa assumed a carefree expression. ''Oh, no, sir. Nothing to do with you, sir. How could it possibly have anything to do with you?''

There was a further tightening of his facial muscles, a fleeting look of puzzlement—or irritation—jetting across his brow. ''I don't understand you at all, Stockton. When did you make the decision to cancel?'' he shot at her.

''Last Sunday night. Before I—''

''Why?''

Tessa shrugged. ''Well, if you must know, sir, I found my fiancé in bed with another woman.''

''Hell!'' he said, astonished.

''That was, to put it mildly, the beginning of the end,'' Tessa said.

He made a contemptuous sound, straightened up and strolled to the window. Tessa turned in her chair to look at him. There was an angry cast to his face. His mouth had thinned. The view was giving him no pleasure. He was probably vexed because she had put a spoke in his cosy little plan for the weekend.

Goaded by his dismissal of all the pain she had felt over a man to whom she had devoted four years of her life, however foolishly, Tessa cynically asked, ''Are you feeling any better now, sir?''

''Worse,'' he bit out, not looking at her.

''There are always other women,'' Tessa said derisively. ''There seem to be plenty of them around, willing to take their chances.''

He gave her a sharply mocking look. ''Never the right ones.''

It hurt. Even though she knew she wasn't the right woman for him, it still hurt. "Sorry I failed you, sir," she said flippantly.

"You didn't fail, Stockton." His mouth curved into an ironic smile. "You were very good for me."

It was some balm to her wounded soul. "Thank you, sir."

The memories were back in his eyes, burning into her again. Tessa's pulse started to act erratically. She was beginning to have trouble breathing. Her mind dictated that she had to get away from him. Fast. She pushed herself up from the chair before her legs went all watery on her.

"I'll go now, sir."

"Stockton..."

She wrenched her eyes from the simmering seduction in his and turned toward the door.

"Miss Stockton..."

"Goodbye, sir." She sliced the words quickly at him, and forced herself to walk, one foot in front of the other.

"Tessa..."

The soft caress of her name curled around her, holding her still.

"I'm asking you, very nicely... please, would you reconsider our, er, arrangement?"

Tessa did not look back. She took a deep breath, stiffened her spine and held fast to a sane sensible course. She was not going to be anybody's floozy on the side. Not even Blaize Callagan's. "No, sir," she said firmly.

"Let's get straight to the point. Why not?"

"I'm not interested in casual sex. Nor affairs. Not on a long-term basis," she stated decisively.

"I see."

She gathered her nerve to face him and turned, chin high, a fierce pride blazing from her tawny gold eyes. "I hope so, sir."

He looked at her speculatively, as though she was something entirely new to him...interesting. "So, you're leaving me to my own devices," he softly drawled.

"I'm afraid so, sir," Tessa answered loftily.

He raised an appealing eyebrow. "Nothing I can do?"

"No, sir."

His mouth moved into its sensual quirk. "You don't like me much, do you?"

She gave him a mocking smile. "I guess I'm cautious, sir."

"You think I'm not to be trusted."

Tessa tilted her head to one side consideringly. "I must confess...I wondered, when you were married..."

"If you're asking was I faithful to my wife, yes, I was. I had affairs before I married, and I've had affairs since. I'm a man who likes sex. And a lot of it. But I've never made a practice of mixing women. And I'm very careful about whom I mix with."

"I've noticed, sir."

He winced at the derision in her voice. "You were the exception to the rule."

"I guess I should feel flattered."

His mouth twisted sardonically. "Regardless of what you think of me, I do have a few principles that I live by."

She returned an ironic smile. "Oddly enough, sir, although you may not believe it, so do I."

His eyes gleamed a rueful appreciation as he walked slowly towards her. "I caught you at a vulnerable time, didn't I?"

She tensed, her eyes glinting a hard warning at him. "Yes, sir, you did," she said flatly.

"On the rebound."

"More or less."

He kept coming. "I won't say I'm sorry, Tessa."

It seemed important to hold her ground and stand up to him . . . no matter what! "It was my decision as well as yours, sir."

"That's why you cried," he said softly.

Tessa flushed. Her eyes burnt with a bright defiance as she replied, "Not precisely, sir. I guess you could say a few things caught up with me."

"No regrets, Tessa?"

"I am sorry if I disappointed you, sir."

His eyes mocked her as he slid his arms around her waist and drew her into a loose embrace. "You know damned well you didn't disappoint me. And I won't accept that you don't want anything more to do with me. We're good together."

"In bed, sir. That's all."

"That's a start." He pulled her closer to him, bringing her body into electric contact with his.

Little quivers ran down her thighs, but Tessa found the presence of mind to press her hands against his chest and push herself back, putting some space between them. "More like a finish, sir."

"Not for me it isn't."

Her eyes flashed fierce determination. "I happen to want more than sex from a man, Mr. Callagan."

"Are you implying I can't give you more?"

"You only want my body."

"All weekend?" His slow smile taunted her. "True, I do want it. I'm also impressed by your belief in my virility. But every man needs a breather now and then. Apart from which, I enjoy other pastimes as well, and I'm inviting you to share them with me."

"Like what?" she scoffed.

"Fishing. Swimming. Eating. The occasional word passed in companionship. Basking in the sun. I definitely, most definitely do not want to use your body any more than I want you to use mine."

"Yes, you do."

"Not at all. I concede only that I want to make love to you from time to time, beguile our senses..."

"I'm going home. I have a wedding to cancel."

"I'll cancel it for you."

"It's something I have to do myself."

"All right. Do it tonight. It can't take all weekend. I'll pick you up in the morning."

"I'm going to Gosford. That's where my parents live. And this is something I can't rush. I owe it to them."

He heaved a deep sigh and contemplated the stubborn pride on her face. "I want to kiss you senseless, but I have a feeling you wouldn't like it this time. It's a losing tactic, isn't it?"

"I wouldn't advise it, sir."

One eyebrow rose in appeal. "Definitely a losing play?"

"Yes, sir. Let's just keep the good memories."

"Stockton, I have a terrible weakness for challenges."

"You might get hurt, sir."

"Ah! What do you do when you run into an im-movable object and you don't want to get hurt, Stock-ton?"

"You sidestep it, sir."

"Good memory, Stockton."

"Yes, sir."

"Excuse me while I sidestep."

He dropped the embrace—much to Tessa's relief. If he had kissed her she wasn't at all sure she wouldn't have weakened in her resolve. She watched him shak-ily as he stepped to the desk, scribbled something on a card, then came back to her and handed her the card.

"My telephone number. Ring me when you've fin-ished cancelling the wedding. What is left of the week-end we will spend together."

Tessa looked at him sternly. "Don't hold your breath, sir."

"Something I ought to tell you, Stockton." The dark eyes gleamed with ruthless purpose. "I never give up on something I want."

"Funny you should say that, sir," she retorted. "Neither do I."

She swung on her heel and marched towards the door.

"Nice legs, Stockton," he said appreciatively.

She opened the door before sending him a derisive look. "Thank you, sir. And may I say..."

She paused deliberately. It gave her a thrill of real pleasure to see the look of hope flash into his eyes.

"Yes, Stockton?"

"Your legs aren't too bad, either."

She grinned at his surprise, then made a fast exit on her note of triumph.

It occurred to her, on the way down in the elevator, when her wild exultation calmed down to a mere simmer of excitement, that maybe her mother was right in some circumstances. Maybe saying no did draw a man on. If the man was like Blaize Callagan.

The card he had given her was burning a hole in her hand.

CHAPTER EIGHT

TESSA'S PARENTS lived at Green Point, on the outskirts of Gosford. Fortunately Tessa had caught an express train so the journey had only been a little over an hour. She caught a taxi from the railway station. The sense of impatience, almost urgency to get the issue of Grant Durham over and done with had a lot to do with Blaize Callagan's card in her handbag, but Tessa kept telling herself she would only be jumping out of the frying pan and into the fire if she let herself get involved with *him*.

No future there.

Nothing but bed and possibly breakfast. Occasionally. When it suited him.

She had to be absolutely off her brain to even hope that there was a chance of a real commitment between them. Just because he made her blood sing and she had got the better of him a few times didn't mean his interest would stick beyond the gratification he found with her.

It was a pipe dream.

Sheer pie in the sky.

She was brought sharply down to earth when the taxi pulled up outside her parents' home. It was a well-presented home with neat lawns and gardens, comfortable and solidly middle class.

Tessa was proud of what her parents had achieved, and proud of the independence she herself had achieved. She simply wasn't a match for a high flyer like Blaize Callagan. That was reality, and there wasn't any future in indulging fantasies.

She paid off the taxi driver with a heavy heart and walked down the path to the front door with a dirge-like tread, knowing that the music she had to face was going to be unpleasant. She rang the doorbell and waited, resigning herself to the inevitable in more ways than one.

The door was opened by her mother. She was, as always, neatly dressed in conventional clothes, her hair conventionally permed into rigid waves and curls, lipstick in place, a strand of pearls around her throat, and absolutely everything about her appearance just so. She looked at Tessa, looked past her, then asked, "Where's Grant?"

It had taken Joan Stockton only a few seconds to assess the undeniable fact that Tessa had arrived at her parents' door alone. Grant's car was not in the driveway. Grant was not beside Tessa. Hence, Grant was not here. Her expression instantly became disapproving. Joan Stockton never reacted well to anything that didn't match up to her sense of what was right and proper.

"He won't be coming," Tessa said bluntly.

Chagrin mixed with the disapproval. "I cooked that lasagne he likes especially for him."

Typical, Tessa thought. Her mother's outlook was that men had to be indulged to keep them firmly caught. Except the indulgence didn't run to free sex. "I like it, too, Mum," she said. "It won't go to waste."

She kissed her mother's cheek and pushed through the hallway to greet her father.

He wrapped her in his arms with his usual bear hug. He was an affectionate father, and an indulgent one. Tessa hugged him back fiercely, wishing she could find a man like him.

Grant had decided not to come last weekend, supposedly because Tessa was working on the wedding arrangements with her mother. Although it was plain now that he had had an ulterior motive for staying in Sydney. However, there was absolutely no excuse for his absence this weekend, as Tessa knew. And her parents knew that, as well.

Her father drew back, a look of concern on his weatherbeaten face. He was still a strong man at sixty-five, but his face was deeply lined. He looked his age, although Tessa maintained he had worn well. His iron-gray hair was as thick as ever, and his warm sherry-brown eyes always looked young to her.

"Anything wrong, sweetheart?" he asked perceptively.

"A long hard week, Dad. I had to go to a conference," she said brightly, and proceeded to regale her parents with censored details of the three days she had spent at Peppers.

This lasted her through dinner. After the washing-up was done, her mother cleared off the dining room table and brought out the wedding invitations. Tessa looked at them glumly, knew that prevarication could not be prolonged, sat down at the table and plunged to the heart of the matter.

"Mum... Dad..." She looked at both of them in desperate appeal. "I've got something to tell you. I'm sorry, but there isn't going to be a wedding. I've told

Grant, and we've broken up. I won't be seeing him any more."

Her father reached over and squeezed her hand. "I'm sure it's for the best," he said softly.

Her mother gaped. Her face coloured. She glared at her husband. "Mortimer, how can you say that? How do you know it's for the best? How do you know anything?"

Mortimer Stockton had worked as a carpenter all his life, a plain simple man with a very loving heart. From the moment he had set eyes on Joan Stockton he had adored her, and his philosophy was very simple. His wife knew best, and she was always right. He never argued with her, and agreed with all her opinions. Over the years, this had led to a very one-sided relationship. That didn't save Mortimer from frequently being wrong about things.

He shifted uneasily in his seat. He had been on the receiving end of his wife's diatribes many times in his life, and now lived by the motto, "Peace at all costs." But his youngest daughter was very dear to his heart, so he made one very cautious statement in her defence.

"Joan . . . I never thought Grant Durham was good enough for Tessa. He didn't treat her right. I'm glad she's decided not to marry him," he said quietly.

"Not good enough!" her mother shrieked. "At least he was good enough to want to marry her when he didn't have to! Who's going to have her now? She's ruined herself . . ."

It went on and on. A torrent of recriminations was heaped onto Tessa's head; all her past sins, all her shortcomings as a daughter and as a woman. No decent man would want to marry her. She was wilful and wayward and she had made herself cheap. And now she had thrown away her only chance of redemption.

For once, Tessa felt no inclination to fight back. She didn't try to express a contrary point of view. She sat numbly through it all. She was grateful for her father's efforts to calm his wife down and mitigate the things she was saying, but it didn't really help. It only set her mother off on new tangents. As far as Joan Stockton was concerned, this was the final straw, the ultimate letdown. Tessa was a total write-off. Her only saving grace was the fact that she wasn't pregnant. Or was she?

The negative reply fuelled another barrage on Tessa's attitudes and loose living habits. She could only come to a bad end. No one would ever care about her or for her. A dark future, Tessa thought, her mother's words adding their weight to the sense of empty desolation inside her.

Eventually her mother declared it was impossible to talk to her. Intransigently unreachable. A lost cause. If Tessa had any sense in her head she should call Grant Durham and beg him to take her back. It was her only chance of leading a decent life.

Then she stormed off to bed.

Tessa sat on at the table, white-faced and tight-lipped. Her father sat on with her, his kindly face creased in deep concern, his eyes begging forbearance.

"Your mother doesn't mean those things, Tessa," he said quietly. "She's upset. That's all. The wedding meant a lot to her."

Tessa shook her head. "I've always been a disappointment to her, Dad. I guess I always will be."

He squeezed her hand. "Not to me, sweetheart."

He had always called her his little sweetheart princess, and somehow the affectionate term meant a lot just now. "Thanks, Dad," she said, choking.

"There, there, sweetheart. It's going to be all right. You'll see," he soothed. "You mother means well. Sometimes she just gets a little bit upset. But you're a grand girl. There'll be many a man who'll want to marry my little princess."

"I don't know. I don't think I know anything anymore, Dad. All these years... maybe Mum's right... and all I've done is mess up."

"No, Tessa. Don't think that, sweetheart." He coughed apologetically as he made the most defiant statement of his married life. "Things aren't sometimes as straight and as narrow as your mother would like to have them."

"Mum didn't even ask me why I'd changed my mind."

"Don't you worry. Everything will be all right," Mortimer said vaguely. There were limits to how far he could go in opposing his wife. He could see a lot of storm clouds gathering.

"I guess I shouldn't come home for a while," Tessa said despondently. "Let the dust settle."

"I love seeing you." His eyes were troubled. His was a terrible dilemma.

"Maybe if I got engaged to someone else..." Tessa sighed. It was the only redemption her mother might accept. Unfortunately it could be a long time coming, if ever.

"Don't go running from the frying pan into the fire," her father warned anxiously. Things could get very black if Tessa made another mistake.

Her eyes searched his in desperate appeal. "You don't think I'm bad, do you, Dad?"

"No, Tessa. You're definitely not bad." He shook his head. Why did these things happen?

"What do you think I should do?"

"About Mum?"

"Yes."

Mortimer pondered the matter. "It might be a good idea for you to go back to Sydney in the morning. Give it time for all this to blow over. Your mother will come around. Just a matter of time, sweetheart."

She nodded. The lump in her throat was too large to circumvent.

"You go to bed now," her father urged kindly. "You're worn out. A good sleep. Things always look better in the morning."

Tessa stumbled from her chair, threw her arms around her father's neck and kissed his forehead hard. "I love you, Dad," she choked out huskily.

"There, there, now. It'll be all right. You'll see," he soothed, his voice gruff with emotion.

Tessa went to bed but she didn't go to sleep. She felt very mixed up in her mind, emotionally drained, and as close to complete despair as she had ever come. She had been blindly infatuated with a man for four years. Both her sister and her father had seen him far more clearly than she had. Grant had not treated her right, and she had taken it from him and come back again and again for more, even to the point of marrying him. How could she ever trust her judgement again?

And Blaize Callagan had to be another wrong choice.

Yet he had a lot of qualities that Grant hadn't had. He was honest, for a start. She had no delusions about what he wanted. He had spelled it out. No frills. But he had implied that he hadn't found anyone else who gave him what she did. Which put her ahead of a lot of other women.

Maybe there was a chance with him. Or more likely that was just a delusion because she wanted so desperately to be loved. Perhaps she was one of those foolish women destined always to choose the wrong man.

Nevertheless, despite the high tension between them this afternoon, she had enjoyed sparring with him. He had enjoyed it, too. He hadn't found her ordinary at all. She had piqued his interest. Got under his skin. Maybe she wasn't foolish.

Blaize had made his own luck with the Japanese deal. Wasn't it possible that she could make her own luck with him? Her father was right. Life wasn't as straight and narrow as her mother wanted it to be. Tessa wished it was. There was certainly nothing straight and narrow about Blaize Callagan. He was a very complex man. Then she remembered that he had said she was complex, too. It brought a smile to her face, the first smile since she had left him this afternoon.

Why not, she thought. As far as her mother was concerned, she was a ruined woman anyway. A weekend with Blaize Callagan was hardly going to ruin her much further. If she was as badly ruined as her mother thought, she couldn't actually be ruined any further. She had already achieved a hundred percent ruination.

Besides, she should know by the end of the weekend if any future was feasible with Blaize Callagan or not. Better than closing the door without giving it a chance.

What was the alternative? Wallowing in dark emptiness for a long miserable lonely weekend until she could get back to work Monday. It might be stupid, but suddenly a weekend cruising down the Hawkesbury River seemed a lot better idea. It might lead somewhere, and then again it might not. If she didn't go she would never know.

A bad end, her mother had said.

She was probably right, Tessa thought.

Even so, for better or for worse, it was her life to do with as she chose.

She switched on the bedside lamp, got out of bed, picked up her handbag, extracted Blaize Callagan's card and went to the living room with a purposeful tread. The house was in darkness. She switched on the light. It was almost midnight.

A heady recklessness was upon her. So what if she woke Blaize Callagan up! If he wanted her, he wanted her. Let him suffer for it. She was through with suffering for a man. This time she would dictate the terms.

She picked up the telephone and dialled the number he had written down. It rang three times before the receiver was picked up at the other end of the line. His voice was not at all sleepy. "Blaize Callagan," he said crisply.

"Not in bed?" she asked.

"Stockton?"

"My name is Tessa," she said with pointed emphasis. No more Stockton. If Blaize Callagan wanted her, he could toe the line she set.

He laughed. It was a soft laugh with a warm ring of pleasure in it. "Yes, of course," he murmured. "Definitely Tessa."

Her heart leapt in exultation. Another point won. "I trust you have a good memory."

"Excellent."

"I wouldn't like you to forget what my name really is."

"Trust me."

That was a tall order. On second thoughts, he hadn't said anything he hadn't meant so far, Tessa reminded herself. "I'm coming back to Sydney in the morning."

"It will save time if we meet at Akuna Bay."

"I don't know how to get there."

"I'll send a car to pick you up and bring you to the marina. What's your parents' address?"

She told him. There was a pause while he wrote it down. "It's always good to get an early start. Will eight o'clock suit?" he asked.

"Fine," she said, smugly pleased that he had asked her instead of telling her.

"Mmm...I guess I can attribute this change of mind to my not-too-bad legs."

"You may have a few other good points," she said airily.

"Like what?"

"I'll think about it, see what I can come up with."

Again he laughed. "Tessa...you have just made my weekend."

"Don't be too sure of that...Blaize," she said daringly. "There's many a slip 'twixt the cup and the lip."

"I'll try to please."

"I wouldn't like to be riding at anchor the whole weekend."

"Rest assured you shall have everything."

"I do have a mind, as well," she said dryly.

"We'll explore it together—" a slight pause "—darling."

"Do you get onto such intimate terms with all your women so quickly—" a sense of wickedness made her add sweetly "—darling?"

"I swear this is the first time it's ever happened in my life. Are you in bed?"

"No. Are you?"

"Yes. I was thinking of you. A very bad case of emptiness. Worst I've ever seen."

"Willing me to call?"

"Yes. It worked, too," he said smugly.

"Oh, I wouldn't bet on that, darling Blaize. Maybe I just feel like some distraction."

Silence. Then... "Been having a hard time of it, Tessa?" he asked softly.

"Not easy," she admitted.

"You want another interlude."

"Perhaps." She didn't want him too certain of her. She didn't want to be taken for granted ever again.

"Am I being used?" he asked musingly.

"Yes," she retorted.

"We'll go on a journey of discovery together."

"Sounds reasonable."

"We are in agreement then. Good night, Tessa. I'm looking forward to tomorrow."

"So am I."

"Don't change your mind."

"There's no one else in my life to change it over."

"Keep it that way."

"I'll try." He had better try, too, she thought, or they would reach the end in very quick time. She didn't have another four years to waste on a man who didn't give her what she wanted.

"Sweet dreams," he said softly, seductively.

"Good night," Tessa said offhandedly.

She set the radio alarm by her bed for seven o'clock. She lay awake for quite some time, imagining Blaize in his bed. It made her body tingle. Her mother was undoubtedly right. She was wayward, wilful and wanton, as well, but she was going to try her luck with Blaize Callagan. If it came to a bad end, it did. If she could waste four years with Grant Durham, she could waste a weekend on Blaize Callagan.

Eventually she fell asleep. She woke to music on the radio. Her parents were already up. She could hear them talking in the kitchen when she dashed into the bathroom for a quick shower. Her mother's voice didn't sound quite so strident this morning. She hoped she wasn't going to be subjected to another scene over breakfast.

Tessa dressed in white jeans and a yellow T-shirt. She put her hair up in a ponytail. She didn't want it blowing everywhere once they were on the water. She didn't bother with any makeup at all. If Blaize Callagan wanted to be part of her real life, he could accept her as she was. Without frills. Fortunately she kept an old bikini at her parents' home so she stuffed that into her bag, zipped it up, then carried it out to the hallway near the front door.

She braced herself for another possible onslaught, then went out to the kitchen to face her parents. "Morning, Mum...Dad," she said breezily, heading straight for the cupboard that held the breakfast muesli.

"Good morning, Tessa," her father replied, looking up from his newspaper and giving her a smile.

"Good morning, Tessa," her mother said stiffly.
"Do you want coffee?"

"No thanks, Mum. I'll just have a plate of cereal and
then I'll be going." She quickly poured some muesli
into a porridge plate and headed for the refrigerator to
get the milk.

"Going?"

"Yes." She flashed her father a look of appeal.
"Dad said he'd do the necessary cancellations. And
since I'm only upsetting you further..."

"I have every reason to be upset, Tessa."

"Yes, I know, Mum. I'm sorry. Truly I am. But I
can't marry Grant." She poured the milk over the
breakfast cereal and returned it to the refrigerator.

"Why not?" her mother demanded.

Tessa looked at her mother and knew she would
never understand. Grant's infidelity was beyond her
comprehension. In fact, even if she accepted it as truth,
she would probably blame Tessa for it anyway. But she
was not going to be satisfied without a reason, so Tessa
gave her one.

"Because I'm in love with someone else, Mum," she
said quietly. It was probably a stupid thing to say, but
she just couldn't stand any more recriminations.

Her mother's jaw dropped open.

Her father looked up from his newspaper, eyes
sparking with keen interest.

"You've got someone else?" her mother squawked.

Tessa shrugged and sat down at the kitchen table,
opposite her father. "It might not come to anything,
Mum. But I'm going out with him today. In fact, he's
sending a car for me at eight o'clock so I'll have to
hurry with breakfast."

She quickly scooped up a spoonful and started eating.

"Sending a car? What do you mean, sending a car?" her mother demanded.

"That's what he said. So I expect a car will turn up for me at eight o'clock," Tessa said offhandedly.

"Who is *he?*" her father asked.

"The boss of CMA, Dad. Blaize Callagan. I filled in as his secretary at the conference," she explained.

"Ah!" he said. "Taken a shine to you, has he?"

"It seems that way, Dad."

"How could you fall in love with him?" her mother accused more than asked.

Love? Tessa paused for a moment to consider that question. Was she in love with Blaize Callagan? The thought hadn't occurred to her before. Perhaps she was. And that was why her body reacted to him...and her mind. Certainly she was very strongly attracted to him in every sense there was. But her mother would never understand that. Better to say something that she could relate to.

"Well...he's the most handsome man I've ever seen. And the smartest." Tessa refrained from saying the sexiest. And that in some ways he appeared to be caring and nice. Apart from being a challenge and ...

"How old is he?"

"Thirty-six."

"Is he married?" Suspicious. Expecting the worst.

"Widowed."

Visible relaxation. "How serious is he about you?"

"I don't know."

"Why not?"

"He's never told me."

"Tessa, you can't play fast and loose forever."

"No, Mum. I'm not going to. Cross my heart."

Her mother relaxed a little bit more. "Where are you going?"

"He's taking me out on his boat."

"Alone?"

"Yes, Mum. Alone. He wants to get to know my mind. We're going to explore it together."

"Well, you make sure he doesn't get to know anything else, Tessa," her mother said with a hard look.

"Yes, Mum." After all, he could hardly get to know what he already knew.

Tessa absorbed a barrage of advice. It was better than a barrage of abuse. Her father just smiled. Tessa ate her cereal. At five minutes to eight, her mother took up a vigil at the front door to see what kind of car would arrive for her hopelessly wayward daughter. At precisely eight o'clock, she almost had an apoplectic fit.

"Good heavens!" she choked. "It's a limousine. A white stretch limousine." She recovered fast. "Tessa, are you sure you can trust this man?"

"I hope so, Mum," Tessa said, grabbing her bag for a quick exit. She had to say one thing for Blaize Callagan. He had a lot of style. Almost enough to silence her mother. Except it probably wouldn't last.

Her father came to have a look at the car, as well. Not many white stretch limousines were seen at Green Point. A chauffeur alighted from the driver's side and headed down the driveway.

"Well, 'bye, Dad," Tessa said, giving him a quick hug. "Thanks for everything. Thanks for listening."

"Take care of yourself, Tessa," he said, his forehead creased with concern.

"Not to worry. Everything will work out okay," Tessa assured him.

She gave her mother a quick peck on the cheek. "Sorry about everything, Mum."

"Be a good girl," her mother called after her, more in hope than belief.

The chauffeur took her bag and saw her into the limousine with deferential courtesy. Tessa sat back in the plush leather seat and wondered about the wages of sin. Nevertheless, if Blaize Callagan thought he could seduce her with his wealth, he had another think coming!

All or nothing, she decided.

No compromises.

No half measures.

The weekend would settle what they wanted from each other, and how much they wanted it. If it wasn't enough to get serious, then there'd be no more. If it was enough to get serious, Blaize Callagan would have to rethink his future, because Tessa was finished with grey areas.

White or black.

White, in Tessa's opinion, was for brides.

Black was for emptiness.

And she wouldn't be filling Blaize Callagan's emptiness for long if he didn't want white. The issue was cut and dried in Tessa's mind. Her mother wasn't wrong about everything. It was just that Tessa had to take a slightly crooked path to get to the straight and narrow with Blaize Callagan.

CHAPTER NINE

TESSA HAD NEVER CRUISED the Hawkesbury River. She had passed over it thousands of times in the train, or on the expressway, travelling between Gosford and Sydney. She had always thought it awesome. Wooded hills and stone cliffs rose almost perpendicularly out of the water, the remnants of a river valley that had been submerged by the sea aeons ago.

It had a primeval feel to it, a timelessness that man could never make any real impression on. In some places houses clung precariously at water's edge, but no one could ever tame this wilderness. Boats scythed through the waterways. But the majesty of the fiords made everything else seem unchanging, puny and irrelevant. Even Blaize Callagan's magnificent motor cruiser.

The white stretch limousine had prepared Tessa to expect luxury on the water, and that was a fair description of Blaize's boat. Sheer extravagance from stem to stern. All the latest technology combined with streamlined comfort. Blaize hadn't yet shown her the stateroom, but Tessa knew that was only a matter of time. She had no doubt it accommodated his every material need, as did the galley and the saloon.

He was able to drive the boat from the sun deck on top, and that's where they were, the wind blowing on their faces, sun shining its summer warmth on them, the light glittering off the small waves coming in from the sea. Tessa had a delightful sense of freedom from all care.

"It seems as though you could lose yourself here forever," she remarked musingly.

Blaize smiled at her. "Great idea! They could make a movie about us. *The Man Who Never Came Back.*"

Their eyes clung for a few moments—wary, searching, wanting—then looked away. Tessa wondered what kind of game Blaize was playing with her. He seemed subdued, but Tessa wasn't sure if he was being artful or genuine.

He hadn't placed any pressure on her at all. When he touched her it was only for fleeting moments, nothing she could object to. A touch on her shoulder, her waist, her arm—innocuous really, but it made her shiver.

She knew as well as he did why he wanted to spend the weekend with her. For the moment, it apparently pleased Blaize Callagan to pretend otherwise. He seemed to accept her need to feel free. But Tessa had seen his body language in action before, and she knew how crafty he could be.

He wore well-fitting white shorts, his legs very much on show. His navy and white sport shirt had a collarless V neck and short sleeves. Tessa was very conscious of his body and all its latent virility. It made her very conscious of her own body and every feminine part of her.

"I'm glad you're not a chatterer," he said.

She slid him a mocking look. "I thought you wanted to explore my mind."

Again the dark eyes fastened onto hers, holding them in a sharp passage of intimacy. "I am. Silence can

be just as effective a form of communication as speech.
You are enjoying yourself, aren't you?''

"Yes."

"You don't need to talk if you don't want to."

"Fine."

He nodded and turned away, picking up his mug of
beer to take a sip of it. He hadn't drunk much. Neither had Tessa. He had made her a gin and tonic before coming up to the sun deck and she had barely
touched it. Not through any sense of caution. She
simply hadn't thought about it. The pleasure of the
boat trip, being with him, was quite heady enough for
Tessa.

They cruised idly through the jigsaw puzzle of waterways, finding a remote bay, which looked as though
no man had visited it in the last two hundred years. A
small beach, stands of angophoras, iron barks and the
odd blue spotted gum lending their shade to the hot
sand.

They had a picnic lunch, drank a bottle of wine, and
in the stillness of the afternoon, they lay on a blanket
underneath the trees, replete, relaxed and drowsy in the
softly dappled sunshine. Blaize played idly with her
hand, his long supple fingers stroking through hers,
interlacing, interlocking.

"You have delicate hands," he said. "Quite dainty."

"Yes," she agreed. They *were* fine-boned, small.
Like the rest of her. A sharp contrast to the tall model
he had married.

"Very feminine," he said.

"Thank you." She was glad he liked them.

He rolled onto his side, looking down at her face as
he lifted her hand to his mouth and ran her fingers
slowly over his lips.

This is it, Tessa thought. Am I in love with him? How did one define love? Where was the dividing line between being in love and not being in love? Or was it possible to be partly in love and partly out of love?

She could feel her tension rising as he began to caress her, her temples, ears, throat. His lips followed his fingertips, softly seductive, knowingly erotic. She forced herself to relax, but her heart wasn't in it. Where did it lead? Did she love Blaize Callagan?

It was a strange thing, life. When it hadn't mattered what Blaize Callagan thought of her, she had been free of all inhibitions. Now it meant something to her...

He lifted his head sharply, the dark eyes seriously questioning. "You're not responding."

Her throat was tight but she forced herself to speak lightly. "Perhaps I ate too much for lunch."

"And the real reason?"

Relentless, ruthlessly demanding, slicing through any prevarication. Honest.

"Perhaps I like you making love to me too much, Blaize," she said softly.

"So?"

"It makes it hard to turn away."

He frowned, the dark eyes boring into hers with more intensity. "If I make love to you, you want it to be permanent?"

"Something like that. I guess I don't want to become involved in a situation where I can't win."

He nodded. "I can understand that."

His gaze dropped to her mouth, seemed to study the line and shape of it. Then he bent his head and brushed his lips gently over hers in tingling, tantalising sweeps. Tessa put her arms around his neck. Maybe, if she wasn't already in love, she was rapidly falling.

She let him persuade her lips apart. Or maybe they parted of their own accord. He kissed her, sensuality giving way to hungry passion. Tessa could feel her defences melting as desire surged through her, making her feel utterly helpless. How did one resist an irresistible force? Once in the grip of it...impossible not to be swept away. The only answer was to avoid it. Which wasn't possible this weekend.

"I want to make love to you," he said huskily.

No future promise...just now. "You can if you want to," she whispered.

She could feel his strong desire, the electric tension in him. All her nerve ends were tingling in response to it, strung tight, waiting, wanting.

His eyes burned into hers, their command oddly blurred by a need she couldn't define. He drew in a deep breath and slowly released it.

"I don't think I will," he muttered, more to himself than to her.

"Why not?" she asked curiously. It was why he had brought her here. She had given her consent. What was stopping him?

His mouth curled sardonically. "Do you want the smart answer or the serious answer?"

"What's the smart answer?"

His eyes mocked the curiosity of hers. "Time's on my side."

Relentless, she thought again. Relentless and ruthless in going after what he wanted. He had warned her. But she had meant what she had said, too. He could have this weekend *his* way. But no more after that.

"And the serious answer?" she asked.

His expression slowly changed to one of rueful self-mockery. He lifted his hand and stroked her cheek with a tenderness that seemed at odds with his character. "I don't want to hurt you," he said softly.

Her heart turned over. She was in love. Stupid, really, but irreversible. She wished that just for once, Fate would be kind to her, but it was almost certainly a vain wish. Yet maybe there was a slim chance...if Blaize Callagan didn't want to hurt her. That meant he cared, didn't it?

He hadn't cared about hurting her that first night at the conference. It had been all take then. With a nominal bit of asking. But he hadn't known about her cancelled wedding then. He had thought it was simply a case of mutual desire.

Tessa remembered his vexation yesterday. He hadn't liked thinking it was a rebound effect instead of something strictly between them. And he hadn't liked her crying.

She suddenly realised why he had been standoffish this morning, treading cautiously, waiting. He wanted her to respond to him. Only him. He didn't want her remembering any other man. And he didn't want her to cry afterwards. He wanted her to be happy with him.

Which did show consideration. Certainly it was tied up with his wants, but he was not the taker she had thought him to be. He genuinely wanted to give her pleasure. He had definitely been considering her feelings. Unlike Grant Durham.

"Come on," he said, heaving himself onto his feet. "Let's clean up here and go cruising."

They went to the boat and packed their lunch things away in the galley. Tessa didn't mean to be provocative. She didn't quite know how it happened. She was thinking how nice it was to be with a man who didn't mind cleaning up things and putting them away, who didn't expect her to do everything. The easy companionable way he shared the chore was so natural, as though they had been doing things like this together all their lives. And somehow her eyes couldn't help feasting on him, the lithe economical way he moved, the male beauty of his face, the perfect proportions of his body so powerfully filled out . . .

"Stockton."

She looked up, surprised by the harsh rasp in his voice. "Yes, sir?" she replied automatically, forgetting that he wasn't supposed to call her that.

The dark eyes blazed raw desire at her. "I do not have a strong nobility streak," he grated. "If you keep looking at me like that . . . Oh, to hell with it! I want you!"

He tipped the glass he'd been washing in the sink. He tore the towel out of her hands and tossed it away. He scooped her hard against him and plundered her mouth with an urgency that ran through Tessa like an electric shock, igniting a response that shattered all inhibitions. She wanted him just as fiercely . . . wanted him with a desperation fed by all her unanswered needs.

He leaned against the sink, drawing her with him, moving her in between his legs so that she was trapped by his powerful thighs, so that she was intensely aware of his arousal as he kissed her mouth, her face, her throat, with a fast feverish passion that allowed her no respite for thought. When he paused for a moment to lift off her T-shirt, his face was dark and brooding, his eyes glittering a searing challenge into hers as he tossed the garment away.

"Stop me if you want to," they said, "but you'll be lying if you deny me."

Tessa was not about to deny him. Her excitement was far too high to be doused, and the intensity of his need for her was like a wild intoxicant coursing through her blood.

He unfastened her bra and tossed it away. Lifted off his shirt and tossed it away. The muscles of his chest pulsed to his harsh shallow breathing as he cupped her breasts in his hands, moulding the soft flesh to his touch. His thumbs dropped to the underswell, his fingers splaying out beneath her arms as he slowly drew her to him, brushing her aroused nipples over his chest, easing her more and more against him, savouring the feel of her warm flesh giving, spreading over the firmness of his.

He threw back his head and a raw groan tore from his throat. His arms wrapped tightly around her, crushing her to him. He tipped her head back and once again his mouth ravished hers, stoking his desire and hers to screaming point.

She was barely conscious of their move to the stateroom. They fell onto the bed in a tangle, their bodies rolling. Her hands scrabbled through his hair, kneaded his shoulders, scraped over his back as his mouth worked its sweet devastation on her breasts, every movement a pulse of sharp pleasure. They squirmed out of the rest of their clothes, loath to lose any body contact, revelling in every touch of their heated flesh, sensitising each other to fever pitch.

Their coming together was another soaring into exquisite satisfaction, need chasing need, higher and higher, deeper and deeper, the spiralling turbulence finally exploding into ecstatic fulfilment. But best of all, for Tessa, was holding him afterwards, hugging him to her, stroking his hair, his back, indulging herself in sweet pretence, letting the need she felt flow through her and express itself in tenderness, while he was too drained of strength to move. She didn't think of the future. Or where this was leading to. It was enough to hold him clasped to her, to feel his heart thudding against hers, to own him . . . a little.

Eventually he stirred and levered himself up to look into her dreamy golden eyes. He won't recognise what I'm feeling, she thought. He won't see what he doesn't feel himself. So she stared at him without any attempt to disguise the deep well of emotion he had tapped.

He brushed his fingertips around her temple while his eyes studied hers as though they were strangely foreign to him. Then he bent and kissed her softly before moving away. Tessa did not try to hold him. Nor follow him. She knew instinctively that clinging would be anathema to him. He was a man who made his own decisions, who went his own way.

But he did not lie on his back, separate and apart from her. He propped himself on his side and idly trailed his fingers over her stomach as he studied her face some more. There was no tension in their silence, more a peaceful stock taking of where they were now.

"Would you consider coming to live with me, Tessa?" he asked.

It surprised her that he had made the leap from casual lover to a live-in situation. It meant that he wanted more of her than he had first indicated. But she wasn't going to fall into the grey area again. Once was enough.

"No," she said firmly.

There was no reaction on his face. Blaize Callagan gave very little of his inner thoughts away. He simply watched her intently, assessingly. "Any particular reason?" he asked after a short pause.

Tessa shrugged her shoulders. "You...living with one of your secretaries? You'd want to hide it, Blaize. Downplay it. Degrade it. I don't blame you for that. It would only be natural. But it's not for me. I'm not good at playing second fiddle to anyone. Not even you."

He nodded his head. His brow creased in thought. "So we keep meeting like this."

"I don't think so."

Again a cautious pause. Then lightly, "Any particular reason?"

"I don't want to spend my life waiting for you to fit me into yours from time to time."

"I'd make them good times, Tessa."

She shook her head. "A string of fantasies, Blaize. I want real life. And I want a man who'll share that real life with me. What you're suggesting would only put me on hold from what I'm looking for."

He gave that quite long consideration before he spoke again. "So this is our first weekend together, and our last."

Tessa bravely hid the painful stab of disappointment she felt. No chance with him...ever. Of course, she had been foolish to think there might be. Men like Blaize Callagan simply did not get serious about women like her. Pie in the sky.

At least she had stuck to her guns and not crumbled into compromises and half measures. She could be proud of herself on that score. She had faced up to the future and not made a foolish choice. Which left her only this weekend with him. One night and another day to indulge what could be the love of her life.

She knew what he wanted from her—to be happy with him—and she wanted that, too, for the short time she would have him. She smiled, her golden eyes lit with hopeful appeal. "Let's make it beautiful, Blaize. Happy and beautiful."

For a fraction of a second he looked puzzled. Then he smiled at her. "Agreed. Happy and beautiful."

And it was happy and beautiful. It seemed that the decision having been made, they both relaxed their private guards and did precisely as they pleased, making the most of the brief time they had together. If Tessa felt like touching him she did, and Blaize enjoyed the same freedom, neither one rebuffing the other at any time. Tessa found it intensely pleasurable to just follow whatever whim took her, often teasing Blaize into surprised laughter. The sense of sharing grew more and more intimate as all inhibitions fell away between them.

When they made love that night, Tessa asked Blaize to hold her afterwards. She told him she liked being cuddled. He seemed to enjoy obliging her. He cuddled her until she went to sleep, and when she woke up in the morning his arm was still around her waist, her body snuggled spoon fashion against his. The moment she moved, his arm tightened around her, and they made love again before getting up.

Sunday was a perfectly glorious summer's day. They had a swim before breakfast—skinny-dipping, which was something Tessa had always wanted to do but never done. It was a deliciously sensual experience, made even more so by being with Blaize. He was an incredibly exciting lover, unpredictable and very erotic. He certainly hadn't lied about being a man who liked a lot of sex. But Tessa didn't mind. She found she liked it, too. A lot. With him.

After breakfast they did some fishing for a while, with no success. Tessa thought they probably weren't concentrating on their lines enough. Occasionally she caught Blaize looking at her in a wondering fashion, as though he didn't understand what was happening or why, but he liked it. He definitely liked it. The warm pleasure in his eyes was not feigned. Nor was the amusement. He enjoyed being with her.

By mutual consent they spent the last of the afternoon in bed. They made love to each other, and Blaize held her for a long, long time, not moving apart, lying joined together even when his aroused state was gone. It was beautiful. She felt happy and sad . . . happy for what she had had with him, sad for the inevitable end to it. She snuggled closer, kissed his throat.

"Thank you, Blaize," she murmured huskily. "Thank you for being good to me."

He made no reply. The fingers threaded through her hair tightened their grip for a few seconds, then slowly relaxed. He sighed. "It will be dark soon. I guess we'd better start moving."

They cruised slowly towards Akuna Bay. Blaize had the motors barely turning over. The shadows lengthened as the sun started to sink behind the mountains. The flaming clouds changed to a deep purple. Blaize didn't seem to be concerned about the gathering darkness. The boat puttered on.

"We'll take forever to get back there at this rate," Tessa commented dryly. They could have spent longer in bed together, she thought regretfully.

He reached out and curled his hand around hers. "Do you mind?"

"No." She wasn't going to mind anything. Happy and beautiful to the end, she decided.

"Neither do I." His dark eyes seemed fathomless in the twilight, but she had the impression they were filled with good memories. "I like this speed," he murmured.

It was nice that he felt reluctant to part with her, Tessa thought. She laid her head on his shoulder. His arm slid around her waist, pressing her closer to him. A mood of melancholy wrapped them in silence. Twilight had fallen. The birds had gone to bed. There was a pale moon rising, a week older than when she had last seen it at Peppers. She wondered what Blaize was thinking.

He cleared his throat.

"Stockton..."

Ah! It was over. Back to business, Tessa thought with resignation. Time for the switch off. She didn't know how Blaize did it. Although she guessed it was relatively easy when one's emotions weren't deeply involved. She was glad she had decided against any further "weekends" with him. They would have killed her.

"Yes, sir?" she drawled mockingly.

A long pause. She had the impression of furious mental activity. There was definitely a rise of tension in his body. His chest rose and fell on a long-drawn-out breath.

"Stockton, I'm not in the habit of making hasty decisions."

"No, sir," she recited flatly.

"So this decision—you'd better believe it—is not hasty."

"Yes, sir."

"Stockton, I'm going to marry you."

Tessa's mind went totally blank with shock. She had given up any hope of that remote possibility. She was resigned to the inevitable parting. She couldn't take it in.

"Why, sir?" she asked, unable to believe it.

"Because I want you, Stockton."

Good heavens! Tessa thought. I really did force him into black or white by refusing all the grey areas. But she had never really anticipated he would want her that much. With the prospect in front of her, she suddenly thought of all the reasons he shouldn't marry her. She was not another Candice. She would probably be a total misfit in his world. And after he had been satisfied with the pleasure he obviously got from her, where would they be then? He would begin to look critically at her. He would start thinking she didn't measure up. And that would be dreadful. Dreadful!

"No, sir," she said in a very small voice.

"Stockton, did I hear you correctly?"

"Yes, sir."

"Give me one good reason we shouldn't get married," he demanded tersely. He was even more tense now.

Tessa was feeling very tense herself. "We wouldn't be happy together, sir."

"Don't be a fool, Stockton. Marriage has got nothing to do with happiness."

She gaped at him. He looked steadfastly ahead, grim-faced with determination.

"Then what has marriage got to do with, sir?"

He switched off the motors. The cruiser drifted idly along the middle of the Hawkesbury River. He turned to her, lifted his hands onto her shoulders. He had a weary look on his face. He spoke in a tone of infinite patience.

"Tessa, marriage is about *need*. It's about two people needing each other. You recognise that. You need me. I need you. To the exclusion of everyone else. It's really that simple."

Tessa looked at him blankly. She had never thought of it like that before. In a way he was right. Grant had said he loved her, but he had never *needed* her. Not exclusively. And then there were her parents. Poles apart, but each leaning on the other for their needs. Sue and her husband... There were others. A long list of them. And this new perspective fitted them all.

"Perhaps you're right, sir," she said.

"Of course, I'm right. We need each other. Exclusively. We get married. Simple." There was a ring of deep satisfaction in his voice. Problem solved.

No, it wasn't, Tessa thought. For one thing, she didn't like his switch-on switch-off inner mechanism. That had to stop if she was going to marry him. He had given her what she wanted this weekend. Having experienced that, she wasn't going to accept anything less. Why should she? Surely a wife was more important than a weekend lover.

She looked up at him defiantly. "I don't think you would like my conditions, sir."

"Like what?"

"You will treat me lovingly all the time," she stipulated firmly.

One eyebrow rose. "Regardless of how I feel?"

"Regardless of how you feel. Lovingly. All the time."

"What kind of deal is that? Where's the compromise?" he demanded.

If he thought he could make their marriage a business deal, he could think again, Tessa thought furiously. How could she have fallen in love with such an impossible man?

"There's no compromise, sir. That's the deal!"

He frowned. He turned dark brooding eyes to the shoreline. It was obvious that he didn't like being cornered. He was probably weighing up how much he wanted her against how much he didn't want to put himself out, Tessa thought cynically.

He seemed to brace himself as he turned to her. "I can do it," he said decisively. "I can do anything I set my mind to. Of course, I can do it."

His hands fell to her waist and he started kissing her forehead, trailing his lips around her temples as he drew her closer to him.

"There are a few other minor problems," Tessa said.

"I'm showing you how loving I can be," he murmured, planting warm kisses on her hair.

"You're arrogant and overbearing..."

"Trivial," he scoffed, nuzzling her ear.

"Demanding and impatient..."

"What does that matter?" He transferred attention to her nose, kissing the tilted end of it.

"Thoughtless and self-centred..."

"Details," he said. "Mere details." And closed her eyes with more gentle kisses.

"Uncaring of what others think and feel..."

His head jerked back. "Now you've gone too far," he said sternly. "That is not *true.*"

"Isn't it?"

"No." His gaze dropped to her mouth. "I care a lot about how you feel when I do this." He tilted her head so he could kiss her on the lips. It seemed to last forever. Not just sensual, although it was certainly that.

Loving. He had to want her an awful lot, Tessa thought with a deep thrill of pleasure.

Was she in love? Well on the way, she thought. Just the slightest bit more encouragement and she could be head over heels. She kissed him with all the fervour swelling from her heart.

He leaned into her, moaning his desire.

"We could go below," she suggested.

He took a very deep breath. His eyes glittered with triumphant satisfaction. "And leave this boat floating around the river? That's irresponsible. You'll have to learn to control your desires, my girl."

Tessa laughed at the payback for making him control his desires. "Yes, sir," she said mockingly.

"And stop calling me 'sir.' Use your memory bank, Stockton."

"Yes, darling Blaize."

"Say you're going to marry me."

"Are you going to stop calling me Stockton?"

"I only did that to concentrate your mind along the right path. You've been saying quite a lot of nos that I haven't liked. When you say you'll marry me I'll call you Tessa darling. So are you or aren't you? Be damned if I'll ask you again!"

She took a deep breath. Her mind was singing silly exultant songs. Her heart was pitter-pattering all over the place. "I think I must be crazy," she said slowly, "but yes, I think I will."

"Right!" he said grimly. "And don't think I'm going to let you slide out of it. When I want something, Tessa darling, I get it. One way or another."

He kissed her once more as a firm promise of that, then turned aside and switched the motors to full throttle. They roared to the marina. Tessa wondered if he was impatient to take her to bed again, but once they were docked, he hurried her off the boat and over to the car park where he quickly bundled her into a streamlined white Lamborghini.

''Where are we going?'' she asked as he climbed in beside her.

He grinned. Jubilantly smug. ''To your parents' place. We are going to uncancel a wedding. A six-week engagement will suit me just fine. And naturally I intend to get your parents' blessing.''

Tying her up. With bows, Tessa thought. She suddenly had a sinking feeling their marriage wouldn't last very long. Blaize probably had no scruples about divorce. Relentless and ruthless, she reminded herself. He would have what he wanted from her for as long as he needed it ... and then what?

Tessa heaved a deep sigh.

She would just have to take her chances and make the most of them.

At least, for a while, she would be redeemed in her mother's eyes.

CHAPTER TEN

BLAIZE MADE NO COMMENT on her parents' home. He helped her out of his car. The gull-wing doors were somewhat startling—not what Tessa was used to—but she hastily reminded herself that she was plunging into a lot of things she wasn't used to in marrying Blaize Callagan.

Was she really going to marry him?

The determined look on Blaize's face said he knew what he was doing. Tessa wondered if she knew what she was doing.

She realised, as Blaize hurried her down the path to the front door, that where and how her parents lived were totally irrelevant to him. They could have occupied a shack in the outback for all he cared. Probably her parents were irrelevant to him as well. Only one thing was relevant. Getting what he wanted. Signed, sealed and delivered. And tied up with pretty bows.

Her mother answered the doorbell, undoubtedly puzzled over who might be calling at such a dreadfully late hour. It was almost ten o'clock. She saw her wayward daughter first and instantly froze. "Tessa," she said. "What have you done?"

Then she saw Blaize. Her mouth remained open but no words came out. After all, Tessa reasoned, her mother liked men to be handsome. Blaize Callagan was probably the most handsome man she had ever seen. He did have this effect on women.

Tessa herself was still being strongly affected by him. Very strongly. He claimed he was faithful to one woman at a time, and he had better stay that way, she thought grimly. She had a few ideas of her own on how that could be accomplished.

Tessa took a deep breath and got on with introductions. "Sorry it's so late, Mum, but this is Blaize Callagan, and he doesn't work by the clock. He wanted to meet you and Dad. He thinks now is as good a time as any. In fact, he wouldn't consider any other time, so it's not my fault. Blaize, this is my mother, Joan Stockton."

"My pleasure, Mrs. Stockton," Blaize said, flashing his dazzling smile as he offered his hand.

Joan swam slowly out of shock. "Oh, dear, oh, dear, oh, dear," she gasped. Her hands went to her hair to primp, in case the permanent wave was not just so. Then she touched her lips in horror at the thought her lipstick might have faded. Her hand dropped to her throat. "And to think I've already taken off my pearls."

"You look fine, Mum," Tessa assured her, knowing how much it meant to her mother to always look her best.

Tessa was distracted by an oddly grateful glance from her mother. With a bit more firmness in her manner, Joan managed at last to take Blaize's hand. "Well, uh, you'd better come in, Mr. Callagan."

At least her mother hadn't quite melted on the spot, Tessa thought. Of course, that wouldn't have been right or proper. Joan Stockton fluttered, waving an invitation, and Blaize instantly got Tessa moving into the house.

She gave her mother a quick hug on the way to the living room. "It's okay, Mum," she whispered. "You're looking good. You always do."

"Thank you, Tessa." She sounded truly grateful.

Her father was in his favourite armchair, watching a Sunday night movie on the television. "Mortimer..." her mother warned stridently. "You won't believe this, but we have a visitor."

He looked up, saw Tessa and Blaize, and hurriedly rose to his feet. "If you like," he suggested brightly, "I could turn the television off."

His wife confirmed that the idea was a good one. "Yes, Mortimer, do that."

He stabbed his finger at the remote-control device on the armrest of his chair, straightened up then looked questioningly at his youngest daughter.

"Dad," Tessa began again. "This is Blaize Callagan. My father, Mortimer Stockton."

Her father looked Tessa's new man up and down as Blaize stepped forward to offer his hand. Her father wasn't the same with other men or women as he was with his wife. From a man he would never take a backward step. Only his adored wife had any right over the way he thought and how he thought it.

Tessa was proud of her father. He might have been a carpenter all his life, but he was a true craftsman with all the confidence and dignity that being a master of his job gave him. He took Blaize's hand strongly, but he did look somewhat overwhelmed by the presence of the man who had come among them.

But she had won today, Tessa reminded herself with deep satisfaction. She had set the terms and Blaize had gone for the white.

"Mr. Stockton," he said warmly. "I realise this is a rather late hour to be calling on you . . ."

"It is a bit," her father managed. "But where Tessa is concerned . . . well, that's fine."

"Very well said, Mr. Stockton. It's what I expected of you." Blaize was putting on his most genial soothing manner. Tessa had seen it at work during the mealtimes at the conference. "Tessa has to come first," he said. "That's precisely what I thought. I'm glad we agree about that."

Which surprised her mother and father no end.

"Well . . ." said Joan Stockton uncertainly. She had never thought like that and she couldn't see where it was leading to.

Blaize took over. "I understand from Tessa that you've had an upsetting weekend. With the cancellation of the wedding." He shot a sympathetic look at Joan Stockton. "That was too bad."

"Oh, very bad," said Joan.

"So I thought it best not to waste any time correcting such a distasteful situation," Blaize said helpfully.

Joan Stockton looked confused. "What can be done?" She slid into one of her nervous anxiety moods. "There is nothing that can be done," she answered herself rhetorically.

"Oh, yes, there is, Mrs. Stockton," Blaize assured her. He turned to her husband. "Mr. Stockton, there are a lot of fools in this world, but I'm not one of them. I want to marry Tessa. I've come to ask for your permission. Tessa has consented to marry me, and I'd like your blessing on that. And yours, too, Mrs. Stockton. I want to get this right, straight from the start."

He flashed his dazzling smile.

Tessa saw her mother go weak at the knees.

"Oh, dear, oh, dear, oh, dear." She fanned herself. She was definitely suffering a hot flush.

Mortimer glanced at his wife for help. Joan Stockton was beyond giving it. She was totally bewildered. All her sacredly held principles on how a woman should act had been shattered by Tessa. She didn't know whether this new marriage proposal was the work of the devil. Mortimer Stockton got no help from his wife.

He took a momentous decision. For the first time since he was married, he took an independent stance. He looked hard at Tessa, refusing to be swayed by the man at her side. "Well, sweetheart, do you want this man, or are you being railroaded into marriage?"

Tessa had to tell the truth. It meant too much to her father. "I guess it's a bit like you and Mum, Dad. I *need* him."

Mortimer Stockton nodded sagely. He understood that. His eyes lifted to the man his daughter needed. "Then, Mr. Callagan...Blaize...it's fine by me," he said firmly.

"Thank you, sir," Blaize said respectfully.

Mortimer Stockton relaxed. "Tessa's a good girl," he said.

Tessa smiled. She loved her father dearly.

"I appreciate that, Mr. Stockton," Blaize said, "and she's the right one for me." He drew her forward into the crook of his arm, taking up the stance of a man in firm possession. "Tessa and I are agreed that the wedding should go ahead in six weeks' time. The only difference will be that I'm the groom. If we have your approval.''

Mortimer looked hard at his wife. It had been a hard struggle but Joan Stockton had come to a decision. ''Yes,'' she said, and looked commandingly at her husband. This was certainly for the best. It saved Tessa from a bad end.

Mortimer Stockton gave his approval. ''That's fine by my wife and me.''

Joan Stockton looked as though she couldn't believe Tessa's luck. Tessa resolved never to tell her how that luck had come about.

''Well,'' she said, her face suddenly beaming with approval. ''Let's all sit down. I'll make a pot of tea. Or would you rather have coffee, Mr. Callagan? Or perhaps a drink of some kind? I don't know what we've got,'' she added nervously. ''What have you got, Mortimer?''

''I'm driving, Mrs. Stockton,'' Blaize cut in smoothly. ''Coffee will be fine. Thank you.''

They settled around the dining-room table. Blaize took a keen interest in all the arrangements Joan Stockton had made for the wedding. They had already been to so much expense . . . what could he contribute? He, of course, would supply all the wines and drinks, and he was sure that Mr. Stockton would understand that, in this day and age, the groom's family should and would pay half the wedding costs. Did they think that fair? Tessa's father heartily approved this sentiment. Grant hadn't offered to pay for anything.

At Blaize's encouragement, Joan Stockton took a deeper and deeper interest in the new wedding by the minute. It would be nice to add this or that . . .

Of course, there was a great difficulty in explaining to her family and friends why Tessa would have a new partner for her wedding, but considering all the difficulties of the situation in explaining previously why Tessa had no partner at all, this was most definitely the lesser of two evils. And if the wedding was grander than the original plan . . . well, who was going to think critically at all, particularly when they saw the groom.

Tessa looked on in amazement as Blaize Callagan turned his full charm on her mother, who was reduced to malleable putty in no time flat. By the use of judicious flattery, and the force of his personality and position, he had Joan Stockton eating out of his hand.

The devil, Tessa thought. He can not only charm, but bewitch a woman who is old enough to be *his* mother!

She felt a stirring of resentment. Blaize hadn't wooed her like this. He hadn't used any charm on her at all. Then Tessa remembered Grant Durham's charm and decided she didn't want any more of that. She preferred things the way they were between her and Blaize. Honest and straightforward. She knew where she was with him. She wasn't being fooled into believing that he loved her, so she wasn't going to be let down on that score. He needed her. She needed him. Simple.

But she couldn't help wishing that things were just a little bit different.

"You're so knowledgeable about weddings, Mr. Callagan," her mother gushed. She hadn't yet gained sufficient confidence in the situation to be certain enough in her own mind to call him by his first name.

"I have had one before," Blaize said dryly.

Which reminded Tessa . . . how would she stand up against Candice? What on earth was she taking on?

"Oh! Of course," her mother said. "I forgot." That nonplussed her.

"At this time we don't want to remember it," Blaize soothed. "This is a time to look forward to something happy and beautiful."

"Yes. You're right," her mother quickly agreed, her whole face glowing with approval at this obviously correct attitude.

Blaize asked for one of the wedding invitations, said he would have them all reprinted with his name on them. After all, it was all his fault the arrangements had been altered. He should pay the penalty. He would get them to Mrs. Stockton by Tuesday, along with his list of guests and a social secretary to write them all out under Mrs. Stockton's personal supervision. The secretary could get them posted without delay. It was a pity Tessa wouldn't be able to help but he needed her in Sydney with him. Urgent and pressing business, he called it, without so much as cracking a smile.

But he did look lovingly at her. In fact, he had peppered the whole discussion with a lot of loving touches and glances for Tessa. Blaize had very decisively set his mind on treating her lovingly. I hope this keeps up, Tessa thought.

Her father was most impressed. Her mother was over the moon with approval. Although every time she looked at Tessa there was a sort of glazed look of wondering disbelief in her eyes.

Tessa knew what she was thinking. "How did Tessa get a man like this?" To her mother's mind, Blaize Callagan was, without a doubt, the finest redemption Tessa could have come up with. She was almost saved. In fact, Joan Stockton was beginning to look at Blaize as though he was some kind of Ultimate Being—or at least a special messenger therefrom—because miracles were just pouring out of him.

Tessa wasn't too sure that she wasn't still heading for a bad end. However, only time would tell her that. At least she was on the straight and narrow for a while. She was actually being pushed along it at a rate of knots by the man who was intent on having her, one way or another.

Her parents accompanied them out to the white Lamborghini. Joan Stockton's eyes were like flying saucers. Perhaps she wondered if she was seeing a UFO—or having a special encounter of the third kind. As far as Mortimer Stockton was concerned, any car would have looked like a silver lining. The black clouds were drifting away. His wife would be happy... his little sweetheart princess would be happy... Cars didn't matter at all.

Joan was flustered into silence when Blaize pressed a warm goodbye kiss on her cheek. He took Mortimer's hand again and squeezed it man to man.

"You look after our Tessa now," her father said. Then as a last word on the subject, he added, "Treat her right."

"Like a princess, Mr. Stockton," Blaize shot back at him with fervour.

He couldn't have picked a better phrase. Tessa wondered if Blaize was psychic. It was uncanny how he could read minds. Although he hadn't been able to read hers. Not completely. She reminded herself to keep being somewhat unpredictable. She had to hold his interest somehow.

Her father gave her an extra big hug. "He's all right, sweetheart. No mistake about him," he murmured.

Tessa hoped so.

The die was certainly cast now with her parents brought on side. No way were they going to countenance the cancellation of *this* wedding. That would be complete damnation. Her mother would never speak to her again.

"Happy now, Mum?" Tessa couldn't resist asking as she kissed her mother's cheek.

"For goodness sake, Tessa," her mother whispered urgently. "We can't talk about that *now*. Keep being a good girl. At least until the wedding."

Tessa was happy to see her father looking very content as she and Blaize drove off together. Her mother's approval, unfortunately, had sunk into anxiety again. Tessa could read her expression loud and clear. "Don't stuff up." Except her mother would never say such words. They weren't at all proper.

The Lamborghini began eating up the expressway to Sydney.

"Nice parents," Blaize remarked smugly.

Tessa shook her head. She couldn't imagine any parents in the world looking down their noses at Blaize Callagan. Apart from his natural qualities and his obvious wealth, his performance could not have been faulted. Courtesy, sensitivity, consideration, generosity—and very loving.

She, however, had a little problem. "What about your parents?" she asked, quailing at the thought. Would they accept her as easily as her parents had accepted Blaize?

"I'll take you to meet them tomorrow night," he said, shooting her an appealing look. "Best if it's done before the announcement's printed in the *Herald*."

"You're going to put an announcement in the newspaper?"

He looked sternly at her. "I'm very old-fashioned, and I have old-fashioned values."

Liar, Tessa thought. But he looked so smug and self-satisfied that she didn't argue with him at all. It really was amazing he had taken everything she had said to heart. Mind like a computer, she reminded herself.

"What should I wear to meet your parents?" she asked, hoping they wouldn't compare her too badly against whatever standard Candice had set as a daughter-in-law. Tessa had a sinking feeling that it was an awfully high standard.

Blaize's mouth quirked into that knowing little curve. "I thought that black suit you wore last Monday was very fetching." The dark eyes gleamed briefly at her. "But I prefer your hair down."

"Okay," she agreed. He ought to know best, she thought. Her hair wasn't red-gold, but it did have nice honey tones through the brown. Maybe his parents might like someone quieter looking than the flamboyant Candice.

"You will need a change in status, Tessa," he said thoughtfully. "You can't stay on as Jerry Fraine's secretary."

Good, she thought. She could keep a better eye on Blaize if she was *his* secretary. Make sure his eyes didn't drift anywhere they shouldn't. "What do you suggest?" she asked lightly.

"Oh . . . give up working."

And lose her independence? Tessa brooded on the implications of that for several moments. She didn't like the idea at all. It made her feel too vulnerable.

"Are you going to give up working?" she asked.

"No."

"Neither am I," she said firmly.

Blaize frowned at her. "I certainly don't want you working for Jerry Fraine. The status is all wrong, Tessa."

"I could work for you," she suggested.

"No. Definitely not."

"You need looking after," she argued.

He slid her a mocking look. "We wouldn't get any business done."

"I'll wear my glasses."

"No. No. No. Not those rotten ghastly glasses."

"And I'll put my hair up."

"No." He groaned. "Not that either."

"I'm a good secretary."

"The best I've ever had." He smiled.

"Then why don't you want me?" Tessa demanded.

"I do," he said feelingly. "That's the problem."

"Then I'll get a job with some other firm," Tessa declared determinedly. He wasn't going to dominate her life if she couldn't dominate his!

"I'll think of a way," he said grimly. "But in the meantime, you finish with Jerry Fraine tomorrow."

"Sounds like being fired," she said resentfully.

"Something like that," he agreed, refusing to give an inch on that issue.

Tessa sighed in resignation. He did have a point. Big companies like CMA had clearly defined status levels . . . even to the point of who got into which helicopter. Although Jerry Fraine was a top-level executive, it wouldn't be right for Blaize Callagan's fiancée to be working for him.

In fact, she could see that Blaize would not like to have his wife working in any lowly position. Candice, of course, had run her own business—a very successful high-status one at that—which had been perfectly acceptable. This thought made Tessa feel miserable.

But she was a good secretary.

Tessa was not given to putting herself down, and stubbornly fought the sense of inferiority that Candice's image kept pressing onto her. The only solution that Tessa could see to the dilemma was to be Blaize's secretary. Or personal assistant. That sounded even better. She decided to work that angle when a suitable time came up. Which was not right now.

They arrived at her apartment block and Blaize escorted Tessa up to her door. She wasn't sure, at this point, if she was supposed to ask him in or whether that might contravene the white decision. Her mother had advised being a good girl. But when she opened her door and turned to kiss Blaize good night, he decided the matter for her.

"You know I'm going to marry you, Tessa," he said, taking her into his arms and pressing her body to his with deliberate suggestiveness. "Very soon," he added persuasively.

Don't hold him back?

Tessa struggled with the quandary.

"Are you frightened?" he asked softly, the dark eyes instantly picking up the confused vulnerability in hers.

"A bit," she admitted.

"I'm not."

"You're a man," she said. Nothing much changed for a man with marriage. His life went on along the same course. It was the woman who got forced into giving up things.

"Is there a difference?" he asked.

"Haven't you noticed?" A thread of hard cynicism there.

He sighed. "Do you want me to hold back?"

"Maybe a little bit. Until we're married."

"Okay," he said, then scooped her up in his arms, strode into her apartment, kicked the door shut behind them and found his way to her bedroom as though he had a homing device.

"Do you call this holding back, Blaize?" She meant to sound critical, but her voice came out all husky bemusement as he started undressing her with swift efficiency.

"I won't stay all night," he said.

"Oh. That's all right then," she murmured vaguely as he started kissing her throat on a blissfully exciting downward trail.

Some considerable time later, when Tessa lay peacefully in Blaize's arms, happy and content and tired, she wondered if it was possible to be ruined and saved concurrently. She decided that it probably didn't do any harm to keep Blaize's need for her at the forefront of his mind. Although he had an excellent memory, she didn't want to take any risk of it dimming. And after all, they were now committed to marrying each other. Which did save her from being ruined.

"What will I say to Jerry?" she asked, idly planting little kisses around Blaize's beautiful face.

He looked surprised. "You tell him the truth, of course."

"He's going to be disappointed about losing me as his secretary."

"He'll take it on the chin. He has too much sense to give you any argument about it."

She didn't like to admit she felt nervous about telling Jerry the truth, so she let the subject drop. Apart from which, Blaize decided it was time to distract her again. He had a very high success rate. Tessa wondered how he gathered the energy to leave her, but he did eventually do so, in the early hours of the morning.

"You're a hard bargainer, Tessa darling," he muttered as he got into his clothes.

She had a moment of weakness when she almost said he could stay, but she wanted Blaize to keep respecting her, so she held her tongue. She waited until he was dressed then gave him a long lingering kiss.

"Good night, darling Blaize," she whispered.

"Six weeks is a hell of a long time," he growled, taking his leave darkly.

So is a lifetime, Tessa thought unrelentingly.

She could see a lot of problems ahead.

How she was going to solve them, Tessa didn't know, but she was going to work hard at it. One thing she didn't want was a failed marriage.

CHAPTER ELEVEN

TESSA FELT AT ODDS with herself the next morning when she went in to the office. She regretted having to leave her job. Nevertheless, she had no choice. It was an unavoidable consequence of marrying Blaize.

She liked Jerry Fraine. He had been good to her, and she wanted him to think well of her. It was such an unbelievable announcement that Tessa still felt nervous about it. She hoped they could part on a friendly note.

She started packing up her personal things while she waited for him to arrive. He breezed in at nine o'clock, wishing her the top of the morning from his doorway.

"Uh, Jerry, I need to tell you something." Tessa rushed the words out before he retreated into his office.

"Sure. Come on in, my girl. Bare your breast. Not literally, of course."

Tessa breathed a sigh of relief. He must have had a happy weekend, she thought. He was in a good mood. Which had to help. She followed him in to his office. He sat down behind his desk and lifted his eyebrows expectantly.

Tessa plunged in. "I'm getting married, Jerry."

"Ah!" he said. "Rift healed."

"No." Tessa shook her head. "Not to Grant Durham. I told you that was finished, Jerry." She took a deep breath and spilled it out. "I know this will probably come as a shock to you. Blaize Callagan has asked me to marry him. I'm going to do just that. In six weeks' time. He insists I have to resign. Today, in fact. Otherwise he'll fire me."

Jerry's jaw dropped. He stared blindly at her for several unnerving seconds, then the strangest mixture of expressions flitted over his face—bemused wonderment, rueful appreciation, self-mockery. Finally the faint curl of his lips grew into a broad smile, and a soft chuckle issued from his throat. His eyes started dancing with some unholy joy.

"Jerry," Tessa reproached him. "It's not a joke. I'm completely serious." She lifted her hands in an appeal for his belief. "Blaize has already reorganised the wedding. He really is marrying me. And I'm marrying him."

"I'm sorry, Tessa." He made a valiant effort to clear his throat. "I'm sure it's serious," he affirmed, but although his mouth tried to maintain a serious line his lips kept twitching into an irrepressible grin.

"Then what's so funny?" she demanded tersely, feeling hurt by his reaction. Perhaps Jerry Fraine didn't think she was good enough for his boss.

"Nothing! Nothing at all!" he replied dismissively.

Her tawny gold eyes glinted with hard accusation. "You laughed."

A flicker of discomfort was instantly followed by the adoption of Jerry's best bargaining face. "I've been a good boss to you, haven't I, Tessa? Tried to keep everything pleasant for you?"

"Yes," Tessa acknowledged. "I'm sorry I have to leave you in the lurch like this."

"That's okay! That's fine!" He made a dismissive gesture. "As a last favour to me, don't tell Blaize Callagan that I laughed when you told me the good news."

"Why not?" Tessa bored in, not at all satisfied with the situation. Jerry Fraine was definitely hiding something.

He grimaced an appeal. "Please, Tessa, just forget it. Impulse of the moment."

"I want to know why you laughed," Tessa said with determination. He had aroused a lot of uneasy suspicions with his laughter, suspicions she needed settled.

Jerry Fraine looked at her eyes, the stubborn tilt of her chin, assessed the damage he had done to himself and knew he was fair and square on the horns of a dilemma. Another look at Tessa's eyes and he made his decision. Tessa Stockton had always proven trustworthy, and his best option was to trust her again.

"If I tell you, and you tell Blaize Callagan, it'll be the end of me for sure. You wouldn't do that to me, would you, Tessa? I've got a wife and kids to support," he pleaded.

She heaved an impatient sigh. "All right. I won't tell him anything. But you'd better spill the truth, Jerry. Tit for tat."

"Okay." He took a deep breath, grimaced again, then chose his words with extreme care. "Well, the fact is Blaize Callagan has been, uh, interested in you for quite some time. Months—"

"You've got to be joking!" Tessa scoffed.

"I'm not joking."

She looked searchingly at him. "How do you know that?"

"Because he's been picking my brains about you. What you thought, what you did, how you reacted to things. Everything. He wanted to know everything about you. It was never overt, always subtle, but always there. I knew what was going on. I knew he was going to pursue you . . . when the time was right."

"But . . ." When had Blaize ever noticed her? "He didn't know me," she remarked in puzzlement.

Jerry gave her a wise look. "He knows more about you than you can possibly imagine."

"Then why didn't he do something about it? If he was so interested in me . . ."

"Oh, Blaize Callagan is a master of strategy," Jerry said bitterly. "He would wait until the time was right for him."

Tessa frowned over that remark, aware Blaize did calculate everything to his best advantage. He certainly liked time to be on his side.

Jerry quickly recollected himself and projected an earnest look. "I did my best to protect you, Tessa. I never realised something serious might come of his, uh, interest. So I tried to put the lid on it. I told him you were getting married. Wouldn't even look at another man. But that, quite obviously, was no deterrent to Blaize Callagan."

"Oh!" Tessa did not know whether she was shocked or flattered by Blaize's ruthless disregard for her attachment to another man.

"When the accident happened to Rosemary, he saw his chance. And took it. No doubt if that hadn't happened he would have made some other chance to open the way," Jerry said musingly. "Once that guy makes up his mind, nothing stands in his way."

If it does, he steps around it, Tessa thought.

Jerry paused to project apologetic appeal. "I was called to choose a substitute secretary for the conference. But it was . . . made clear to me that you were the only suitable choice. Not spelled out exactly. But the message was quite unmistakable. I am not known to be slow at picking up inferences. I got the message. After all, I've got a wife and kids to support."

He heaved a rueful sigh. "I regret to say that, although it weighed heavily on my mind, I did put my livelihood ahead of your welfare, Tessa. I hasten to add that, knowing your particular circumstances and your character, I felt if any woman could stand up to Blaize Callagan you were the one. And I prayed very hard that everything would go right."

Tessa remembered Jerry had looked as though he was praying in the helicopter. After Blaize had lifted her bodily into her seat. And he had advised her, too late, on Tuesday morning to keep her guard up with Blaize or she might get torn apart.

"I have always thought you were a grand girl, Tessa," Jerry went on with gathering fervour. "Taken a personal and paternal interest in you. I hope you appreciate—I'm sure you do—that Blaize Callagan is a very hard man to say no to. I just couldn't."

"I see." She gave him a stern look. "You let me walk into the lion's den without so much as a word of warning, Jerry Fraine."

He lifted his hands higher. "Tessa, I swear, I didn't know for certain. I could have been putting two and two together and making five. But the fact is . . . well, to put it bluntly, you do have a lot of femininity . . . and . . ."

"I do?"

Jerry nodded knowingly. "The cutest bottom in the building."

Tessa huffed. "I'm more than just a bottom, Jerry Fraine."

"I know. I know," he said hastily. "And I figured Blaize Callagan would find that out in very short order. At least, I hoped so. I prayed for it."

Tessa now understood why Blaize had looked at her as he did in his office last Monday morning—studying her and giving those little nods of satisfaction. He had noticed her, and wanted her, and when extraordinary circumstances had presented him with a handy opportunity, he had gone for what he wanted. Totally ruthless.

He had known she was getting married. And he hadn't known the wedding had been called off. Was he a complete cad? Well, she was going to find out about that when a suitable moment came.

Jerry grinned. "Obviously you got to him, Tessa. And good for you! I couldn't be more delighted. Thrilled. Without a doubt, what Blaize Callagan needs is a wife like you."

Tessa frowned. Why did Jerry think Blaize needed a wife like her? On the surface of it, she wasn't suitable for Blaize at all.

Jerry suddenly cracked up, peals of mirth spilling from him in uncontrollable bursts. "I just think it's glorious justice that everything's turned out the way it has. The biter got bitten. Well and truly. Not even Mr. God Almighty Callagan could have anticipated that it would all turn out like this."

He took his spectacles off and wiped tears from his eyes. "Or maybe he did. Forget what I just said, Tessa. Maybe he always meant it to. God knows. I've never been able to read him right. Not completely right."

Blaize had meant to have her, Tessa thought. That was absolutely right. However, she was only too aware that it was she who had forced the marriage decision onto him. If she hadn't, would Blaize have ever come to it?

Jerry shook his head. "I was wrong to laugh. It was the surprise of it. That's all. Apart from my wife, you're the most marvellous girl it's been my privilege to know, Tessa. And I congratulate you. With all my heart and mind and soul, I do most fervently congratulate you. You're the only person I know who's beaten Blaize Callagan on a deal and come out winning. A pity you can't stay on. You could have given me lessons."

Tessa couldn't help smiling at him. Whether the winning would go on was a big question mark. She had no idea what the future held. "Why do you think Blaize needs a wife like me, Jerry?" she asked bluntly.

Jerry Fraine was a very shrewd and a very smart man. He paused, instantly sensing it was a serious question, and he gave her the respect of giving it serious thought. "Don't repeat this, Tessa. This is between us. But I think Blaize Callagan needs humanising. I do believe you're possibly the one person who can do it. And, Tessa . . ."

"Yes?"

He smiled in his kindly fashion. "I hope he makes you happy. I don't know if you will be, but I wish you all the best . . . always."

"Thanks, Jerry."

They parted with mutual regret. They had shared a good working relationship. Tessa thought if she had any influence over Blaize, Jerry Fraine would eventually be promoted. She had no concern at all over Jerry repeating this story to anyone, except possibly his wife. Jerry was the soul of discretion when it came to his business life. After all, he had a wife and kids to support.

Humanising...

The idea lingered long in Tessa's mind. She thought over the weekend she had shared with Blaize, remembering how he had relaxed more and more with her. No pressures. No superficialities. No pretences. Just being their true selves. She wondered if it was what had influenced Blaize into asking her to marry him. Maybe his need for her wasn't just man-and-woman attraction after all. He had spoken of need. Two people needing each other. Exclusively. If that was the case, she did have a chance of making this marriage work. Permanently.

She decided to ring up Sue and ask her advice. As far as Tessa could see Sue had a very good marriage, so her sister ought to have a few clues on how to keep a husband happy.

However, when she called Sue she found her mother had already been on the telephone to her older daughter most of the morning, regaling her with the unbelievable news. So Tessa had to give her version of the latest development in her love life before she could get to the point. Eventually the moment came.

"How do you keep a man happy, Sue?" This was most important to her.

"Simple," Sue replied. "No difficulty there. Stay happy yourself. If you're happy, he'll be happy. He won't know why he's happy, but he will be. That's a fact."

It certainly seemed to fit yesterday's experience. She remembered Blaize looked at her as though he didn't know why he was feeling good. Nevertheless, it seemed too easy. Tessa was doubtful.

"Are you sure that works, Sue?"

"Positive."

That was reassuring. "Then thanks for the advice, Sue," Tessa said with sincere appreciation.

"Not advice. Never give it. Statement of fact."

"Thanks all the same."

"Pleasure."

Sue had a lot going for her, Tessa thought. A lot of wisdom. It could be handy for the future. She decided to consult her older sister more frequently.

Tessa put Sue's policy into immediate practice. That night Blaize took her to meet his parents. Tessa did not let herself become nervous and inhibited. She did not let their obvious wealth intimidate her. She was happy to be with Blaize, happy about their forthcoming marriage, happy to meet his parents—who started looking indulgently at her after a while—and happy that Blaize treated her so lovingly. She was, after all, head over heels in love with him, and she didn't care who knew it.

It seemed to have a disastrous effect on Blaize's control. After they made their farewells he drove around the block and made love to her in the car. As always, with Blaize, it was a very interesting and exciting experience. Then he took her to her apartment and made love to her again. Less frantically but with no diminishment of passion.

He was obviously reluctant to leave her, but he forced himself to do so with good grace, merely commenting with heavy irony that he had made a mistake about the wedding. He should have got a special licence. Which assured Tessa that he was still keen about marrying her. Keener than ever.

He took time off on Tuesday morning to take Tessa to his favorite jeweller. None of the rings they were shown satisfied his demanding taste. He commissioned one to be specially designed for Tessa's hand. It had to be dainty, he said. In the end, he settled for a spray of diamonds in a delicate gold setting. Tessa would have been happy to have any engagement ring, but she was delighted Blaize wanted to give her something that would be uniquely hers. It made her feel she belonged to him and that she was unique to him.

"I'll take you to my accountant now," Blaize announced. "He'll fix up a few things for you."

"Like what?" Tessa asked.

Blaize looked uncomfortable. "It's a pro tempore solution. Because I put you out of your job. You'll need money."

Tessa frowned at him. "I don't want your money, Blaize. A good secretary can always get a job. If you don't want me as your secretary—"

"Tessa..." The dark eyes pleaded for forbearance. "Apart from anything else, there is Rosemary to consider."

"You could pass her on to Jerry Fraine."

"That would be a demotion."

"Promote Jerry then."

His eyes hardened. "Are you trying to tell me how to run my business?"

She stared back stubbornly. "I want to be your secretary, Blaize."

He sighed. "I'll work something out. Meanwhile..."

He left her with his accountant, who took her to a bank, and very shortly Tessa was financially richer than she had ever been in her life. She had a personal account and a housekeeping account and was signed up for a stack of credit cards.

She suddenly had access to an enormous sum of money, more than Tessa had earned in all her working years. Somehow she couldn't bring herself to argue with the accountant, which was probably why Blaize had left her with him. But she did feel uncomfortable about it. She suspected Blaize was simply determined on getting his own way again.

Her parents, his parents, her resignation from her job, the announcement in the newspaper, the ring, the money... Blaize was tying a lot of bows fast and furiously.

Tessa remembered what Jerry had told her, and how Blaize had gone ahead and taken her anyway, despite the fact she was supposed to be marrying someone else. Maybe Blaize wasn't as honest as she thought him. Maybe he did whatever was expedient to get his own way. Maybe he was a cad. She recalled his smart answer, "Time's on my side."

Blaize Callagan was a complex man.

Tessa needed to get some straight answers.

Sue had invited them to dinner that night—to look Blaize Callagan over for herself—and Blaize called at Tessa's apartment at six o'clock. He was early, but he said he had nothing else to do. He stretched out on her bed and watched her get ready. He seemed to enjoy watching her, making the odd desultory comment.

It seemed as good a time as any to do a little probing, so Tessa casually asked, "Remember the first time we made love, Blaize?"

He flashed her his dazzling smile. "Vividly."

For a few moments, Tessa thought nothing else really mattered, as long as she had him. But then the question arose again—how long would she have him for? She wanted answers.

"At the time..." She pushed on, then hesitated, wondering how best to word the question without giving Jerry away.

"Yes?" Blaize prompted.

She projected curiosity into her voice. "Did you know I was going to be married?"

He didn't lie. "Yes."

She looked at him, her golden eyes troubled as doubts about his integrity flooded through her mind. "Why did you do it, Blaize?" she asked quietly.

He went very still, the dark eyes scouring hers. "Does it upset you?"

She turned away and went on brushing her hair, not wanting to lie to him. It did upset her. Yet, in another sense, if he hadn't done it, they wouldn't be where they were now. The problem was, she wasn't sure if that was a good thing or a bad thing.

In a fast fluid movement, Blaize was off the bed and taking the brush from her hand. He dropped it on the dressing table and turned her towards him, drawing her into a gentle embrace. The dark eyes burned into hers, demanding that she listen, demanding belief.

"Tessa, you weren't married to him," he said softly. "I wanted you with me, not with some other man." He grimaced in rueful self-mockery. "I wanted to be with you...to know what it was like to be close to you. That first night I wasn't playing around. I hadn't planned it. It...just happened."

He frowned. "Tension. It was the tension that decided it. And you didn't reject me. I'm sensitive to people...to vibrations. You may not think so, but I am. That's why I'm successful at doing what I do. But if you had made one move to stop me, Tessa, I would have stopped."

Would he have stopped? The doubt still lingered in her mind. Blaize went after what he wanted. He had told her so. What the truth of this was, she couldn't tell. "So it was all my fault?" she asked, trying to read his mind.

"No, my darling." He sighed, his eyes appealing for her understanding. "It was my need. I made all the moves. The fault was...is all mine. When I felt there was a chance for me, no way was I going to pass it up without trying. I wanted you, Tessa. And I knew, you see, that the tension wasn't all mine."

"No. It wasn't all yours," Tessa conceded. "The intimacy of the cottage...it was unnerving. And you..."

"What about me?" he asked, his eyes sharpening, probing with urgent intensity.

She felt the sudden rise in his tension but didn't understand the cause of it. She smiled to take it away. "Well, I don't want to boost your ego, but the plain truth is, you are my fantasy-lover material, Blaize."

For some reason her reply increased his tension instead of abating it. His face tightened into a grim expression. However, before he made any response to her explanatory comment, the doorbell rang.

"Are you expecting someone?" he asked tersely.

Tessa shrugged ignorance. "Might be a neighbour wanting to borrow something," she said, and went to answer the summons, quite relieved to have a breathing space to sort through what was happening with Blaize.

It wasn't a neighbour.

It was Grant Durham.

He pushed past her, thrust a page of newspaper in her face and burst into outraged speech. "Is this some horrible joke?" he demanded furiously, eyes glaring suspicion and accusation. "I give you time to cool down and come to your senses, and—"

"Who is this man, Tessa?"

Blaize Callagan's voice whipped down the living room and curled Grant Durham around to face him. Grant gaped at him. As well he might. If looks could kill, Grant would have been slain on the spot.

"My ex-fiancé," Tessa said briefly, extremely conscious of the explosive tension emanating from her new fiancé.

"Tessa is mine!" Grant burst out belligerently. "She's been mine for years!"

Blaize started walking towards him, deadly intent in every step. He was bigger, taller, more robust and powerful than Grant.

"She is not yours anymore," Blaize said very quietly. "You treated her badly. Beyond contempt. You don't deserve her, you filthy gutter scum. You denigrated her. You upset her. You despised what you had."

Grant lifted a hand in protest. "Now hold on a—"

Blaize grabbed the lapels of Grant's suit coat and lifted him off his feet. "If you ever come near her again, I'll smash your head in. And a few other parts, as well. Do you understand that, you slime bucket?"

"Look! You don't understand!" Grant squawked. "I've got a new therapist—"

The expression on Blaize's face, the violence emanating from him in black waves was frightening enough to Tessa, let alone his target. "You worm," he raged. "You heap of green-tinged garbage. I'm going to—"

Tessa had to do something to stop it. There was no doubt what Blaize was going to do, and it was going to hurt Grant a great deal.

"Put him down, Blaize," she appealed hastily.

"Why?" he growled.

"I don't want you to hurt him."

He stabbed a sharp look at her, saw her anxious concern, then with great reluctance set Grant on his feet.

"That's better," said Grant, pretending not to be more than ruffled. "Much more natural..."

"Please go, Grant," Tessa slid in quickly. It was plain stupid of Grant to think he could twig a tiger by the tail. She could feel the coiled tension in Blaize. He was all set to pounce again. The dark eyes were black with barely repressed passions.

Grant perversely tried his luck again, his green eyes projecting the full blast of his lying charm. "I love you, Tessa."

"Truly?" she tested coldly.

"Yes. Above everything else ... I'd do anything for you."

"Do you want me to be happy, Grant?"

"Yes. Of course I do, Tessa," he said with vehement fervour.

"Then I'm sorry, Grant, but I don't love you. And I'm happy with this man. I'm going to marry him. So if you truly want me to be happy..."

"But we've been together so long," Grant argued passionately. "How can you be happy with someone else?"

Blaize growled a warning.

Grant threw a wary glance at him then quickly concentrated on Tessa again. "What am I going to do?"

"See your new therapist," she advised.

"You're going to need a lot of therapy if you don't start moving," Blaize promised him threateningly.

"Yes. I suppose that is the best thing," Grant said nervously. He moved away from Blaize, reached the door, then looked at Tessa, pained bewilderment on his face. "You're really going to be happy with him, Tessa?"

"I'm happy now, Grant," she stated pointedly.

"I'm sorry. Sorry for what I did, Tessa. Sorry I failed you..." For the first time ever Grant looked vulnerable, totally at a loss.

"It's too late, Grant," Tessa said softly. The four years hadn't been all bad. But they were over. "This is goodbye," she said firmly.

He left on a muted half sob.

Weak, Tessa thought. And turned to the man who was strong in every way.

Blaize's eyes were glowing furiously. "You should have let me finish him off."

If anything, his tension was even more pronounced. Tessa sighed to relieve some of her own. The situation had been awkward, to say the least, with her old lover and her new lover confronting each other. "I'm sorry you had to be here," she muttered self-consciously.

"I'm sorry I didn't throw him out the door," Blaize grated.

She lifted appealing eyes to him. "It's over now, Blaize."

His eyes bored at her, wary and watchful. "You did say permanent, Tessa," he reminded her sternly.

"Yes, I did," she affirmed.

"I told you I meant to have you," he said.

"Yes, you did."

"You don't need him."

"That's why I told him to go."

"You need me."

"Yes," she said fervently, realising Blaize was feeling uncertain of her.

"He might come back."

"Blaize, I don't want him back. If he comes, I'll tell him to go again," she assured him.

Still he was disturbed. "Fidelity works both ways, Tessa."

"Yes, it does."

"No changing your mind."

"No."

"I think you'd better come and live with me."

"Are you still going to marry me?"

"Yes," he said vehemently.

"I don't like you not trusting me."

He paused. Frowned. "I do trust you. I just want to protect you."

"Am I going to be your secretary?"

He grimaced. "Tessa . . ."

"I just want to protect you, Blaize."

He heaved a deep sigh. "Well, if you're living with me, I guess I might be able to get some business done during the day. All right. You can be my secretary."

"All right. I'll come and live with you. But you still have to marry me."

"The wedding's set," he reminded her. "If you want, I'll marry you tomorrow and to hell with the wedding."

"No. Six weeks is fine." She couldn't possibly upset her mother again.

"We're agreed then."

She smiled. "I think we have *ringi,* sir."

He relaxed. He smiled. Then began to chuckle. Then to laugh. A look of intense happiness lit his face. He scooped Tessa up in his arms, twirled her around, then paused, his eyes burning into hers. "Just remember the Japanese don't sidestep. It's consensus all the way."

"That's fine by me, Blaize darling." Her eyes danced teasingly. "I've never liked dictatorships."

He growled and kissed her. Tessa wound her arms around his neck and kissed him back. She felt very secure. Maybe it was just male possessiveness on Blaize's part, but it seemed to her that his emotions had been very involved a few moments ago. Although it only took a few moments more before he got very physically involved.

He certainly was a complex man.

Maybe, after they were married, she would be able to get him all sorted out. In the meantime, living with him and being his secretary would surely help her in this task. Except she mustn't tell her mother what she was doing. It would upset her mother terribly.

CHAPTER TWELVE

THE SIX WEEKS seemed to fly by for Tessa. Living with Blaize was vastly different to living with Grant. Blaize owned a penthouse apartment at Milson's Point, which was not far from where she had lived. Not only was the place sheer luxury to Tessa, but there was also the service of a daily maid who came in to do the housework, the washing and ironing, and whatever food shopping Blaize required. Blaize cooked his own breakfast—and Tessa's—and more times than not, they ate out in the evening.

Most weekends they were engaged in a whirl of social activities. Blaize insisted she use *his* money for the extra clothes she needed to fulfil these engagements, and even came shopping with her to make sure she didn't stint on anything. Tessa simply wasn't used to having enough money to buy *anything*. She found it difficult not to keep checking price tags. Blaize didn't so much as blink an eyelid at the cost.

She was deliriously happy with him, and Blaize showed every sign of being absolutely content with her. To Tessa's amazement his friends seemed to accept her without reservation. She decided it was probably because no one had the temerity to criticise Blaize Callagan's choice of wife, particularly since he always treated her lovingly. He was exceptionally good at that. Which just went to prove that when Blaize set his mind on something, he carried through with complete dedication.

He found a position for Rosemary Davies as personal assistant to one of his high-powered friends. The beautiful blonde made no waves about being asked to resign. Tessa was established as Blaize's executive secretary, and she did her best to keep his mind on business.

There were times when he got very tense. Luckily his apartment was only five minutes away from the CMA building. They often took work home with them. Tessa liked sharing everything with Blaize, and he very quickly became used to it. He even went so far as to express the view that it was a good system. Efficient and relaxing.

A week before the wedding there was a meeting of executives in the boardroom. Jerry Fraine remarked that she looked happy. Tessa replied that she was. Jerry smiled at her and slyly added that Mr. Blaize Callagan seemed to be getting more and more human.

The day before the wedding, Tessa went home to her parents' house. Her mother expected it. Besides, Tessa wanted to have one last night with her parents before the final commitment to a new life as a married woman.

Blaize was reluctant to let her go. It almost sounded as though he nursed some suspicion she would get cold feet about their marriage at the last moment if he let her out of his sight. Which was too absurd to credit. Nevertheless, he informed her, before she left him, that if she wasn't at the church on time, there would be dire consequences.

Joan Stockton was in a flutter, checking and rechecking everything, wanting everything to be right and proper and perfect for the big day. Tessa and her father did their best to calm her down. Joan insisted that they each take a sleeping pill so that they would get a proper beauty sleep. Mortimer remarked that he didn't think it would help his beauty, but he took the pill from his wife without any argument. After all, she knew best.

Tessa woke to a stream of beautiful morning sunshine spilling through her bedroom window. A zing of nervous excitement instantly raced through her veins. This was it—her wedding day. By tonight she would be Mrs. Blaize Callagan.

"Happy the bride the sun shines on," she sang in her heart. Her eyes lingered exultantly on the beautiful wedding dress hanging on the door of her wardrobe. The beading on the high collar and on the lace bodice sparkled through the plastic covering. This afternoon she would walk down the aisle in that dress, and Blaize would be waiting for her in front of the altar, and they would be married... *To have and to hold unto death do us part.*

Her wedding day. Tessa could hardly believe it. After all these years this was the day she would marry the man she loved.

A light tap on the bedroom door drew her attention. It was bound to be her mother, Tessa thought, and hitched herself up on the pillows, a smile of greeting already lighting her face as the door opened and her mother's head poked around.

"Ah! You're awake!" Joan said with satisfaction. She bore a tea tray into the room. "It's a beautiful morning. Not a cloud in the sky. Did you sleep well, dear?"

"Like the proverbial log, Mum." She grinned at the tray, which held considerably more than a pot of tea—a plate of bacon and eggs and a pile of toast, all freshly prepared. "Am I being spoiled with breakfast in bed?"

"I thought you might like it," her mother said indulgently. She sat on the bed, her hand automatically lifting to her daughter's face to tuck some wayward strands of hair behind her ear—a small dainty ear, as delicately feminine as her hands and feet. She heaved a sigh and looked at Tessa with troubled eyes. "I just want to say... I've only ever wanted the best for you, Tessa. If sometimes... well, we haven't seen eye to eye about a lot of things... but all's well that ends well. And I hope you'll be very happy with Blaize."

"Thanks, Mum. I'm sorry I've been such a worry to you. I promise you I'll be the best wife I can be, so you won't have to worry any more," Tessa said with deep sincerity. Then she threw her arms around her mother's neck and kissed her. "I do love you, Mum. And thanks for cooking a wedding day breakfast for me. I really appreciate it."

"There, there... You're a good girl, Tessa," her mother said. Which was the equivalent of, "I love you very much and thank heaven you're now saved." She was always flustered by any show of emotion. "Eat up now before it gets cold," she commanded, but there was a blur of tears in her eyes as she quickly withdrew.

It was a happy day. Sue and her family arrived soon after breakfast. Sue was to be matron of honour, and her four-year-old daughter, Jessica, was to be flower girl. The three of them spent most of the morning at a hairdressing salon. In the meantime, Tessa's two older brothers and their families turned up. There was a boisterous family luncheon where her brothers jokingly gave her a lot of advice about how to please a husband, and their wives did quite a bit of correcting them on their opinions.

Sue advised Tessa on her makeup—a touch of blusher to lend an interesting contour to her cheeks, two shades of lipstick to give her lips more definition, a delicate application of subtle eye shadow and a dusting of a very expensive powder that gave her skin a pearly sheen. Tessa was delighted with the result.

The flowers arrived promptly at two-thirty, as arranged. Tessa's bouquet was a long spray of stephanotis that smelled divine. Sue's was a mixture of pink carnations and white roses, while Jessica was to carry the white basket of miniature pink roses.

It was then time to dress. Jessica could barely contain her excitement as Sue zipped her into the sky-blue silk gown with its flounces of lace and threaded ribbons. She looked like a beautiful little doll with the circlet of flowers around her curly fair hair. She raced off to show Grandma and Grandpa, leaving her mother and aunt to their final toilettes.

"I hope she's going to behave herself in the church," Sue said with a rueful smile as she closed the door after her.

Tessa laughed. "She's going to love every minute of it." Then she set about fastening the diamond earrings into her lobes. They were a wedding present from Blaize and matched the design of her engagement ring, five diamonds on a delicate curve of gold.

"They're fabulous, Tessa," Sue said with warm delight. "You sure came up with a prize in Blaize. Perfect husband material."

"You think so?" Tessa was still a little doubtful about that, although nothing was going to stop her from marrying him.

Sue laughed. "Tessa, he adores you. He would die for you."

"I don't know that he'd go that far." Sue didn't understand about how Blaize could set his mind on something and do it.

Her sister raised a challenging eyebrow. "Want to bet?"

Tessa shrugged off the subject with a smile. "No bets." She didn't want to tell Sue that Blaize had never once spoken of love. Not that it mattered all that much. She loved him enough for both of them. She hoped.

She handed Sue a small gift box. "Blaize bought these for you. In appreciation for being my matron of honour."

Sue exclaimed delightedly over the beautiful pearl earrings. "A prize of a man," she insisted again. "He's got taste and generosity."

Sue looked lovely in her sky-blue silk with fitted lace bodice and full skirt. With her blond-streaked hair and artful makeup, she didn't look a day older than Tessa, let alone seven years.

She helped Tessa lift off the plastic covering from the wedding dress, and then held the heavy gown for her to step into it. Tessa carefully fitted her arms through the high puffed sleeves that narrowed to a band at her elbows. She held her hair up while Sue did the zip and fastened the high band around her neck.

Tessa had a long neck and the style suited her, making her look taller and elegant. The top half of the bodice was a fine transparent organza, throwing the rich silk of the puffed sleeves and the beaded collar into sharp relief. The rest of the tightly fitted bodice was beaded lace that curved over her breasts and dipped to a low V below her waist, accentuating every curve of her body. The full skirt was lined with tulle petticoats to make it stand out in a graceful line extending into a flowing train.

Her waist-length veil was short and frothy. It clipped in behind the narrow plait the hairdresser had woven across the top of her head to hold the rest of her thick hair back. Tessa pulled some long tresses forward to curl over her shoulders.

"Perfect!" Sue approved.

Tessa thought so, too. There was a deep special joy sparkling in her eyes. Her wedding day... It was like a dream come true.

There was a tap on the door. "The cars are here," her mother called out. "Are you ready? May I come in now?"

"Yes," both women chorused in eager anticipation.

The door opened. Joan Stockton looked smart and elegant in a tailored suit of shell-pink silk. An orchid corsage dressed one lapel, proclaiming her mother of the bride. Her face was carefully made up to complement her clothes, but her poise was instantly crumpled by a well of tears.

"Oh, my dear!" She came forward and took Tessa's hands, squeezing them lovingly as she shook her head in wonderment and blinked hard. "Is this the baby I held twenty-four years ago?"

"She makes a beautiful bride, doesn't she, Mum?" Sue said with warm pleasure.

"Very very beautiful..." Joan drew in a deep breath and let it out on a shuddering sigh, then at last managed a smile. "I've never felt prouder of you, Tessa."

"Thanks, Mum." Her voice came out huskily. It had to fight past a lump of emotion in her throat.

"Time to go. Your father is waiting at the front door with Jessica."

Sue picked up the bouquets, handed Tessa hers, then fell back to pick up the train of the wedding dress.

Ten minutes later, Tessa was settled beside her father in the back of a white limousine, heading for the church... and her marriage to Blaize Callagan.

"I'm not sure I'm ready to give my little princess away," Mortimer Stockton said gruffly, a film of moisture in his sherry-brown eyes as he looked at his daughter in her wedding finery.

"Sure you are, Dad. That's why you're all dressed up," Tessa teased, struggling to hold on to her composure. She tweaked the pink carnation in his lapel. He was looking distinguished in his light grey suit and pink silk tie, perfectly matched to her mother's outfit, and she loved him very dearly. Her father...about to hand her over to her husband-to-be.

He sighed. "Well, I've got to admit if I have to give you away, I'm pleased that it's to a man like Blaize, sweetheart. I'm sure he'll look after you and treat you right."

"He's been very good to me, Dad," she said truthfully. In fact, when she thought about it, Blaize had done everything she had asked of him. Could Sue be right? Would Blaize do anything for her? Did he adore her? Did adore mean love?

They arrived at the church in good time. A photographer took a spate of photographs. They moved up the steps to the vestibule of the church. Sue made sure the forward section of Tessa's veil was arranged correctly over her face, then fixed the long train so that it would flow perfectly up the aisle. Her father tucked her arm around his. "Ready, sweetheart?" he asked softly.

"Ready, Dad," Tessa assured him with a glowing smile.

The organ inside the church stopped playing a hymn and began Mendelssohn's "Wedding March." Sue raised an eyebrow at Tessa, received a nod, then gave Jessica a gentle push to start her walking up the aisle. The little girl performed as though she was born to it. Sue followed at a stately pace.

Her father gave Tessa's arm a reassuring squeeze. "Now?" he whispered.

"Yes," she whispered, suddenly having an attack of nerves. Her mind frantically dictated instructions. Eyes straight ahead. Smile. Blaize is waiting for you. He chose white. White is for brides. This is your wedding. You can't stuff up now.

But was it right? What if she was making a terrible mistake? What if Blaize never came to love her as she wanted him to?

Her heart seemed to thud heavily in time with the music as they started out. One foot...pause...other foot...pause. Her legs felt very shaky.

Then the man waiting in front of the altar turned to watch her coming to him, and the dark eyes slashed a straight tunnel between them, blocking out everything else. They fastened on her with intense command, driving her heart faster, pouring strength into her legs, drawing her towards him, step by inevitable step.

No release.

For better or for worse, she was Blaize Callagan's bride. And when Mortimer Stockton handed his little princess to the man who had claimed her, Blaize's fingers curled so warmly around Tessa's that it felt as though they were curling around her heart. *To have and to hold from this day forth.*

The ceremony started. Blaize made his responses in a quiet firm voice. Tessa's voice quavered a little over hers, not because she was nervous or panicky any more, but because she felt so much. And the look in Blaize's eyes when he lifted her veil to kiss his new wife...it had to be love, or something very close to it. His kiss was gentle, tender, very loving.

The reception was a triumph for Joan Stockton. The best of everything, everything perfect. Nothing could have been more right and proper. Particularly the bride and groom, who behaved as though the sun and the stars shone out of each other. Joan even allowed herself a little weep when they departed. That was perfectly permissible for the bride's mother, and of course, Mortimer was at her side to comfort her.

Blaize and Tessa drove to Sydney...man and wife. Tomorrow they would fly to Tahiti for a two-week honeymoon on Bora Bora. Tonight they would spend at the apartment. Neither of them had wanted to go to a hotel.

"Happy?" Blaize asked softly as they sped along the expressway.

"Yes," she answered. "It was a lovely wedding, wasn't it?"

He smiled at her. "Happy and beautiful."

Tessa privately wished he hadn't said those particular words. It recalled that first weekend they had spent together—a fantasy weekend outside of real life. She

wondered if that was how he thought of today's ceremony, a white fantasy. He had her now, all his, for as
long as he wanted her. The last pretty bow tied.

No regrets, she told herself.

This was what she wanted, too. Only probably more
than Blaize did.

As if to complete the fantasy for her, when they arrived at their apartment, Blaize scooped Tessa up in his
arms and carried her over the threshold.

"You didn't have to do that," she half-protested.

The dark eyes glowed at her, a warm mixture of deep
satisfaction and contentment. "I really do have old-
fashioned values," he said, then smiled as he kept car-
rying her straight into the master bedroom.

"Be a little patient, Blaize," Tessa chided him. "I've
got a wedding present for you."

"For me?" He seemed surprised.

"I bought it with my money. All the money I'd saved
before I met you." Somehow it was important that he
know that.

He set her on her feet but still held her in his embrace, the dark eyes looking quizzically at her. "Tessa,
I have everything I want. You shouldn't have spent
your money on me."

"I wanted to, Blaize. Wait here, I'll bring it to you."

She hurried to the second bedroom where she had
hidden his gift in a cupboard. She had had it boxed so
he wouldn't immediately know what it was. He had
shed his jacket and tie by the time she returned. He
shook his head bemusedly as she handed him the gift-
wrapped box, all tied up with pretty bows. Tessa waited
impatiently for him to open it, hoping he would appreciate the thought.

But he didn't smile when her gift was revealed to him. He stared at the two bottles of yellow-gold wine, a dark frown creasing his brow.

"I couldn't get the '29 d'Yquem," she hastily explained. "It was too expensive. The best I could do was the '45. I thought two bottles..."

She faltered as his gaze lifted to hers, dark torment in his eyes.

"Did I do wrong?" she whispered, distressed by a reaction that was not what she had anticipated at all.

"Why? Why would you want to remember that night, Tessa?" he rasped. "To give me this tonight..."

He shook his head as though in some dreadful inner anguish. "I've tried so hard to make up for it. I've tried all I could to make you happy with me. I thought..."

The dark eyes searched hers with pained urgency. "I thought today...it was all right. That I'd made the right decision for you as well as for me. Was I wrong, Tessa?"

"No. No... It was right for me," she rushed out with vehement conviction. Her eyes begged a frantic appeal at him. "I don't understand, Blaize. I thought you liked this wine. I wanted to give you something special that you liked."

She felt the relief surge through him even before it hit his face. He stepped forward and swept her into a crushing embrace. His hands ran over her in feverish possession as he rained passionate kisses over her hair. She slid her arms around his neck and pushed her head away enough to look at him.

"Blaize, tell me why you were upset," she pleaded.

His mouth twisted into bitter irony. "Tessa, for me making love with you that night...somehow it went very deep . . . and when you cried, it made me feel like all kinds of a heel for doing what I'd done. It was only then I remembered about the other man in your life . . . but I wanted you so much . . .''

He expelled a long heavy sigh. "When you said you wanted it ended the next morning, I tried to do the decent thing, Tessa, and step out of your life. But I couldn't forget how you'd responded to me. I kept thinking I must have a chance with you . . . that you couldn't be very deeply in love with your fiancé if you could respond to me like that . . . even though you cried.''

"So you called me up to your office.''

He nodded. "And then I realised why you'd let me make love to you. It felt like having my gut kicked in.''

"I'm sorry, Blaize. I didn't think you cared about me,'' Tessa said softly, beginning to realise that his feelings for her ran a lot deeper than she had ever imagined. She reached up and stroked his cheek. "I thought you just wanted a bit of sex on the side.''

"I wanted *you*,'' he said gruffly. "Any part of you that you'd let me have. I thought if I could just stay in your life, given time enough, I could make you mine.''

"I am yours,'' she assured him. "I'll always be yours, Blaize. I love you very much. More than I've ever loved anyone. More than I could ever imagine loving anyone.''

It wasn't at all difficult to say those words with his dark eyes burning with his need for her. Not just need for her body. *Her* . . . the person she was. Why it was so, or how it was so, didn't matter. She *was* the right one for him. Tessa truly believed that now.

"You love me, Tessa?'' he said, half-incredulously.

"That's why I accepted your proposal, Blaize. I fell in love with you that weekend on the boat."

He gave a funny little laugh. "As far back as then? You loved me then?"

She nodded.

"You mean I've been sweating blood to get you married to me, and you actually wanted to marry me all along?" he demanded, his arrogant confidence returning in a burst that blew aside all uncertainties.

"Well, I wouldn't precisely say that." Tessa backtracked. After all, it wasn't good for their relationship for Blaize to be too arrogantly confident of her. He might start taking her for granted. "I wasn't sure that a marriage between us would work. I thought I was taking an awful gamble saying yes."

"You thought you were taking a gamble!" He threw back his head and laughed. Then he picked her up and whirled her onto the bed, pinning her down when she teasingly tried to escape him. "I've got you!" he said. "And I'm not letting you go, so you might as well resign yourself to your fate, Stockton," he said with mock severity.

"I'm resigned, sir. Very happily resigned," she returned cheekily. "But you have to call me Callagan, sir. I got married today."

"Yes. You did." He kissed her. "And don't you forget it."

She kissed him back. "I have an excellent memory, sir."

"Tessa darling, you have a lot to make up for."

"I do?"

"Yes, you do. I worked harder than I've ever worked in my life, thinking of a way to put a proposal of marriage to you. I spent the whole of that Sunday convincing myself I had a chance. I was almost sure you hadn't just been pretending to be happy with me that weekend—''

''I wasn't.''

''—and I couldn't believe that your responses to me weren't genuine.''

''They were.''

''But when it came to the point—make or break time—it was still the most terrifying moment of my life.''

''You? Terrified?''

''Oh, it was all very fine for you, my darling. I wasn't using you as some kind of fantasy lover who couldn't be accepted into real life. You put me through hell!''

''Would a little taste of heaven help you forget, darling Blaize?'' she asked, sliding her hands over him in deliberate provocation.

He growled.

She started to unbutton his shirt.

''You're a witch. You know that?'' he accused, busying his hands on a similar exercise. ''A provocative little witch who cast a spell on me months ago.''

She slid her hands over his bare chest and ran her fingernails over his strongly muscled shoulders. He shuddered. His eyes narrowed threateningly.

''I think I might use one of those bottles of d'Yquem.''

''Well, we'd still have one left,'' Tessa consoled him.

''On the other hand, I don't like to repeat myself.''

''Surprise me then.''

He did. In many and glorious ways. Tessa secretly thought to herself that he really was a fantasy lover, but he made it all beautifully real. Ecstatically real. Afterwards, she even felt brave enough to ask him about his marriage to Candice.

"It was good for its time," he replied. "It was what I wanted then. A very active social scene. Riding high. Maybe we would have grown together."

He fanned Tessa's long hair out on the pillow as he thought about it. "I can't imagine I would ever have had with Candice what I have with you."

"And what's that?" she asked.

"We don't need anyone else," he answered simply. "Like that weekend we had on the boat. It was great . . . just being with each other. And now it's like that all the time for me."

"For me, too," Tessa said softly.

He trailed butterfly kisses around her face. "When did you know that you loved me, Blaize?" Tessa asked curiously.

He gave her a rueful little smile. "Oh, about the time I picked you up to put you in the helicopter. That felt very right to me. This is my woman, I thought. But, of course, I knew you weren't mine. Then the situation changed and I thought I could make you mine. Until you cried that second night . . . and I couldn't comfort you. Because I was the wrong man—"

"You weren't the wrong man, Blaize." She held his face between her hands, and her eyes glowed all her love for him. "I cried because you made me feel so much, and I didn't think you cared for me at all. It seemed so wrong. But it wasn't wrong at all. It was right, wasn't it?"

"Yes. It was right."

He kissed her deeply in the full knowledge of their love and need for each other.

It was their wedding day.

"GET AWAY FROM IT ALL" SWEEPSTAKES

HERE'S HOW THE SWEEPSTAKES WORKS

NO PURCHASE NECESSARY

To enter each drawing, complete the appropriate Official Entry Form or a 3" by 5" index card by hand-printing your name, address and phone number and the trip destination that the entry is being submitted for (i.e., Caneel Bay, Canyon Ranch or London and the English Countryside) and mailing it to: Get Away From It All Sweepstakes, P.O. Box 1397, Buffalo, New York 14269-1397.

No responsibility is assumed for lost, late or misdirected mail. Entries must be sent separately with first class postage affixed, and be received by: 4/15/92 for the Caneel Bay Vacation Drawing, 5/15/92 for the Canyon Ranch Vacation Drawing and 6/15/92 for the London and the English Countryside Vacation Drawing. Sweepstakes is open to residents of the U.S. (except Puerto Rico) and Canada, 21 years of age or older as of 5/31/92.

For complete rules send a self-addressed, stamped (WA residents need not affix return postage) envelope to: Get Away From It All Sweepstakes, P.O. Box 4892, Blair, NE 68009.

© 1992 HARLEQUIN ENTERPRISES LTD.   SWP-RLS

"GET AWAY FROM IT ALL" SWEEPSTAKES

HERE'S HOW THE SWEEPSTAKES WORKS

NO PURCHASE NECESSARY

To enter each drawing, complete the appropriate Official Entry Form or a 3" by 5" index card by hand-printing your name, address and phone number and the trip destination that the entry is being submitted for (i.e., Caneel Bay, Canyon Ranch or London and the English Countryside) and mailing it to: Get Away From It All Sweepstakes, P.O. Box 1397, Buffalo, New York 14269-1397.

No responsibility is assumed for lost, late or misdirected mail. Entries must be sent separately with first class postage affixed, and be received by: 4/15/92 for the Caneel Bay Vacation Drawing, 5/15/92 for the Canyon Ranch Vacation Drawing and 6/15/92 for the London and the English Countryside Vacation Drawing. Sweepstakes is open to residents of the U.S. (except Puerto Rico) and Canada, 21 years of age or older as of 5/31/92.

For complete rules send a self-addressed, stamped (WA residents need not affix return postage) envelope to: Get Away From It All Sweepstakes, P.O. Box 4892, Blair, NE 68009.

© 1992 HARLEQUIN ENTERPRISES LTD.   SWP-RLS

"GET AWAY FROM IT ALL"

Brand-new Subscribers-Only Sweepstakes

OFFICIAL ENTRY FORM

This entry must be received by: May 15, 1992
This month's winner will be notified by: May 31, 1992
Trip must be taken between: June 30, 1992—June 30, 1993

YES, I want to win the Canyon Ranch vacation for two. I understand the prize includes round-trip airfare and the two additional prizes revealed in the BONUS PRIZES insert.

Name _____

Address _____

City _____

State/Prov._____ Zip/Postal Code_____

Daytime phone number _____
(Area Code)

Return entries with invoice in envelope provided. Each book in this shipment has two entry coupons — and the more coupons you enter, the better your chances of winning!
© 1992 HARLEQUIN ENTERPRISES LTD.   2M-CPN

"GET AWAY FROM IT ALL"

Brand-new Subscribers-Only Sweepstakes

OFFICIAL ENTRY FORM

This entry must be received by: May 15, 1992
This month's winner will be notified by: May 31, 1992
Trip must be taken between: June 30, 1992—June 30, 1993

YES, I want to win the Canyon Ranch vacation for two. I understand the prize includes round-trip airfare and the two additional prizes revealed in the BONUS PRIZES insert.

Name _____

Address _____

City _____

State/Prov._____ Zip/Postal Code_____

Daytime phone number _____
(Area Code)

Return entries with invoice in envelope provided. Each book in this shipment has two entry coupons — and the more coupons you enter, the better your chances of winning!
© 1992 HARLEQUIN ENTERPRISES LTD.   2M-CPN